COUNTRY WEDDING

A SWEET ROMANCE

CAROLYNE AARSEN

CHAPTER ONE

"*Y*ou sure you're ready to take on this job?" Kyle looked up from the laptop resting on a table covered with papers and file folders.

A calculator with a stream of paper spooling out of it perched precariously on another set of files.

Derek downed the last dregs of his coffee and set the chipped mug on the counter of the tiny apartment that now served as an office. He'd gone over the numbers until his eyes blurred.

"We need the work. It's been a tough haul the past few years," he said.

Kyle rubbed his hand over his head, his hair slowly growing back after the last round of chemo treatments. Thankfully, the last set had made a difference for him. He had more energy and looked healthier than he had in a while. Which created a flicker of hope in Derek's heart.

"You know what taking this job would mean?" Kyle pressed. "You'd be working for Carly Sutton."

Kyle's concerns echoed Derek's, but reality had to overcome sentimentality and painful memories.

And the reality was the company needed this job to get Crossing Construction profitable. Derek had been gone for the past three years. Kyle and the previous foreman, John Anderson, had done their best, but the company Derek had bought from his uncle five years ago was floundering. The small jobs Crossing Construction had done here and there had helped keep its nose above the ever-rising water, but the bank account was headed toward overdraft territory.

They needed cash flow. They needed work.

And Derek needed to rebuild his reputation.

"It's been over three years since Carly," he said with a shrug that belied his own concerns about working for his ex-fiancée. "We've both moved on. Besides, I probably know her vision for this place better than anyone else."

Kyle's knowing look made him a little annoyed, but he tried not to show it. He pulled a chair closer to the desk and turned the laptop so he could have another look at the spreadsheet. "Have we got everything covered?"

"Not yet, but I've gone over this multiple times with the subcontractors. I think they're getting tired of me."

Derek had to resist patting his younger brother on the shoulder. Kyle had matured a lot in the past three years, which was exactly what Derek had prayed for in the time they were apart.

He had sacrificed a lot for Kyle, but seeing him willing to be involved in the business made those horrible years worth it.

"Okay. Then I'll be submitting this bid."

"You sure you don't want me to do it?" Kyle asked.

"No. I can manage. Print it off and I'll take it over to the Sutton ranch." He'd been back in Millars Crossing for over a month now and though he hadn't run into Carly, he knew it was just a matter of time. May as well get it done and over with. Get the awkwardness out of the way.

Especially if he and Kyle were, by some fluke, awarded this contract.

"Or you could mail it?"

"I want to make sure it arrives on time. We have until tomorrow afternoon to submit the tender, and I don't want it lost in the mail."

"Millars Crossing isn't that big," Kyle said wryly. "Dale just has to take it from the inbox at the post office and put it in Carly's mailbox."

"Doesn't matter. Carly might not check the mail every day."

"And you want to bid on this job sight unseen? You trust what Alex said he's done?"

"Not completely unseen," Derek protested as the printer whirred, spitting out papers. "I had a look at it from the road and yes, I'll have to trust him. He's got nothing to gain by lying to me."

He hoped he sounded braver than he felt. Derek knew he was taking a huge risk, but a lot was on the table and he didn't have much choice. He was sure if he'd asked Carly to show him around the place she would have turned him down flat.

A tendered bid would be harder to deny. Especially because Derek knew they were paring things close to the bone on this. He also knew, talking to Alex Rotko, the previous contractor, that money was tight for Carly. So hopefully they could help each other out.

He fought down his usual resistance, his worries about working with Carly, and yanked the couple of sheets off the printer, and skimmed the figures he knew backwards and forwards.

When the printer spat out the last paper, he gathered them together, tapped them on the desk, and slipped them in an envelope. He was disappointed to see the faint tremor in his hands and hoped his brother didn't notice.

A lot was riding on this job.

But he knew the hardest part of the entire situation would be facing Carly for the first time since he told her he was breaking up with her.

Just before he'd headed off to prison.

The knock on her trailer door broke into Carly's concentration. With a frown, she looked up from the makeshift desk she had put together out of the dinette. It had made the fifth-wheel trailer even more cramped. It also meant that when she wasn't eating at the main house, she was sitting on her bed with a plate balanced on her legs.

All part of the sacrifice she was willing to make to get her event center up and running. Once it was profitable, she could look at building a house.

"Come in," Carly called out, struggling to get out from behind the table tucked against the benches of the dinette. Obviously it wasn't one of her brothers or Katrina or Adele. They would never have knocked and waited. They would've just barged in.

The door opened as Carly scraped her fingers through her hair, wondering who it could be. Salesman? Someone lost?

Whoever it was opened the door but stayed on the makeshift step her brother Wyatt had made for her so that getting in and out of the trailer was easier. This guy was tall, silhouetted against the sunlight, with short hair and wearing a T-shirt tucked into blue jeans. He took one more step into her trailer and she felt a twisting sensation in her gut that spiraled up to her heart. She couldn't breathe. Couldn't think as her world took one spin and almost knocked her back against the bench.

She flailed, reaching behind her to catch her balance.

And then Derek's hand held her arm. Supported her.

He smelled the same, looked the same, felt the same.

She shook off the inane thoughts, jerking her arm away, finding the bench behind her with her other hand.

"Sorry," he muttered, taking a step back.

Swallowing down an unexpected knot of grief, she took a moment to look away. Center herself and catch the breath his presence knocked out of her.

"What...what are you..." She couldn't formulate a coherent thought, let alone question. Three years he had been on her mind. Three years she had fought grief, loss, and abandonment.

And anger.

"What am I doing here?" he asked, finishing the question for her. He moved past her and laid an envelope on the table. "I'm tendering a bid to complete your event center."

"A bid?" She couldn't put her thoughts together in his presence. A presence that took over the trailer, pressing at her.

"Yes. I'm hoping you'll consider it."

She took in the changes the past few years and time in prison had produced. His jaw was leaner, shaded with a stubble that hinted at the rebel he used to be. But his eyes were like flint and his mouth pressed in a firm line. He had bulked up, and she caught the glimpse of part of a tattoo on his right bicep.

The same Derek, but harder.

He still made her heart feel like a hand was squeezing it. Hard. Still pulled the breath out of her body.

She pressed her lips together a moment, holding back a very unwelcome burst of sorrow. *I'm over him*, she told herself. He didn't deserve one more beat of her heart.

She took a breath, keeping her attention focused on the envelope as a way of avoiding his gaze.

"But how do you know what you're bidding on? You haven't been on the property." She probably wouldn't have let him anyway. "How can you know anything about the job? You do realize it's partly done."

He shrugged away her concerns, glancing at the envelope

5

again. "I've been talking to some of the subs who worked on it and managed to snag a copy of the blueprints from your plumber, Nate Brouwer."

"Okay." He obviously had done part of his homework. But there was no way she would consider it. Having him here in the trailer was difficult enough. On the jobsite every day? Not a chance.

"I'll have a look, for sure," was all she could manage.

"Thanks. We put a lot of work into it. I think we could be a genuine contender. Crossing Construction has done some solid work. I believe Kyle and the crew did some work for Katrina."

His sales pitch sounded confident, however, she caught a hint of his previous uncertainty from how his hands were balled into fists at his side.

She wondered if his posture resulted from his time in prison, then shook that thought off. Too many times she had cried herself to sleep, imagining what life was like for him behind bars. Confined. A man who loved nothing more than galloping across the open pastures, hiking trails, and camping outdoors.

But always, right behind that sorrow, was the memory of him walking away from her without telling her anything about what happened. She never heard one word of explanation or excuse from him.

"I heard that," she said.

He took a small step toward the door and Carly willed him to be gone. Willed the tension in her chest to fade away.

"Hey, it's...good to see you," he said.

Really? That's all he could come up with after all this time? After his betrayal?

She lifted her hand. She didn't trust herself to speak. What could they possibly have to say to each other? What could bridge the gap of the years he was gone?

He took the hint and left.

His heavy tread echoed on the wooden step and then faded away. She heard his truck start up and finally she felt like she could relax.

She slid onto the bench of the dinette, her body slack now, a reaction to the tension that had gripped her just moments ago.

Closing her eyes, she pulled in a trembling breath, then another, trying to center herself. She had known Derek was back, and had avoided him for the most part.

The last thing she expected was him coming on her yard, into her trailer, and barging into her life.

She looked over at the envelope lying on the table on top of quotes she had received from other contractors. She had narrowed her choices down to two.

And if she had her way, she would keep it at those two.

No way was she in any way considering a bid from her ex-fiancé.

Ex-con fiancé.

Too easily she remembered the shame and humiliation of having to cancel caterers, florist, and photographer and un-invite everyone when Derek went to prison. But on top of it all, trying to dance around the reason for it. People found out soon enough, however, and whenever she went to town, the looks of pity were often edged with surprise and, at times, a touch of judgment. As if, by extension, she was as nefarious a drug dealer as Derek.

Another knock on her door sent her heart rate into over-drive, but this time she got to the door before it opened.

Finn stood on the step, frowning, his cowboy hat pushed back on his head, his gaze sympathetic.

"Was that seriously Derek Gilbert I just saw here? What was he doing here? What did he want?"

Finn's rapid-fire questions beat at her fragile self-control. But she couldn't let anyone, not even her brother, see how Derek's unexpected and unwelcome presence had affected her.

7

She waved her hand at the envelope on the desk. "He submitted a bid for the event center."

"What? Really? How does he hope to pull that off? And, even more important, how does he have the nerve?"

"His brother still has the construction company Derek bought from their foster uncle. He and Kyle were partners before..." Carly dropped back onto the bench, massaging the pounding in her temples, not bothering to finish the fragmented sentence.

Finn was quiet a moment then stepped farther inside.

"Close the door, please," Carly said. "Don't want to be swatting mosquitoes at one in the morning."

"Sorry," Finn said, doing what she asked. Then he sat across from her and picked up the envelope. "Do you want me to take care of this?" he asked, his voice uncharacteristically gentle. Caring. "I can throw it out for you."

Carly sighed, glancing over at him, then shook her head. "No. I should at least give them the courtesy of looking at it."

"Courtesy." Finn snorted. "I don't know if you should even give him that. Crook. Drug dealer." He spoke the words with such contempt that Carly, who had been the direct recipient of Derek's duplicity, flinched. "You know I never liked the guy."

"That's not true. You warmed up to him after a while."

"Luke-warmed," Finn said with a curl of his lip.

"Let's face it, no guy could measure up to the standards you, Wyatt, and Reuben seem to have for any guy I date. I can't even count how many times I've come home with some guy and he's either a loser, a wimp, a blowhard, ugly, too short, too tall, too much of a jock, too much of a nerd, or some lame reason or another."

"Derek was...sketchy."

His comment dug into the very concerns she held about the man who, against all odds, had stolen her heart.

Once a thief—

"Not always." She stopped herself. She didn't need to defend him. "But he's probably trying to turn his life around now. I imagine three years in prison has to change a man." Which was a thought that had laid heavy on her mind as well once she found out he was back.

Finn shot her a wary look. "You're defending him? After everything he did to you?"

It was technically only one thing, but it was so huge the repercussions of it had reverberated not only through Carly's life, but through the community as well.

It had been Finn and Carly's uncle, Gene Sutton, who had arrested Derek. Uncle Gene had been as shocked as everyone else when he apprehended Derek with two kilos of cocaine in his truck. He was charged and sentenced to four years in prison. And now he was out, probably on good behavior, and hoping to work for her.

"I'm not defending him. Not really."

Finn reached across the table and took Carly's hands in his own work-roughened ones. "Sweetie, I know you've got a soft heart under all that bluster."

"No, I don't."

"Oh, yeah. You cried like a baby when we were kids and we had to give away those kittens."

"Give me a break. I was like, seven."

"Still, softie." Finn grew serious, still holding her hands. "I know you loved him. But I also know how much pain he caused you. You can't trust the guy."

Carly nodded, recognizing the truth in what her brother was saying. And yet...

"I can't believe he changed so much," was all she could say. "When we were dating, he was so loving and kind..."

She let the sentence trail off, wishing she could get her emotions under control. Wishing she could capture the anger she had felt when she first got the news that Derek had been arrested for possession of cocaine.

"He was rough around the edges, you have to admit," Finn said.

Carly gave him a wry look. "You were no saint either."

"Maybe not, but I had the sense to stay under Uncle Gene's radar."

"Literally. I couldn't believe you never got a speeding ticket the way you drove."

"At any rate, Derek and Uncle Gene got to know each other too well. And not in a social sense."

Carly shrugged off his comment. "I know Derek was no saint, but a drug dealer? I still don't understand how he fell that far. I never had any inkling."

"His brother has cancer. I wouldn't be surprised if he was dealing so he could pay for some cure for him. Why else would he do it?"

Carly had entertained that idea many times, and it was the only one that made any sense to her. The only idea that synced with what she knew of the man she had hoped to spend the rest of her life with.

But still...

"There's no way I'd deliberately work with him."

Finn released her hands and glanced over the papers stacked on the table. "Have you figured out who you're choosing?"

The headache she'd been nursing all morning teased her again. "I've got it down to two, but both of them are thousands over my budget. I picked them because they were the least expensive."

"Can you squeeze more money from the bank?"

"Victor told me he had already called in a bunch of favors to get me the loan he did. Doesn't help that anyone I hire will have to work around what Alex has done."

"Call him again. Might not hurt."

Carly didn't relish the idea of going begging back to her account manager. The project was already a month behind schedule thanks to the construction company that had been working on it previously.

And the rain of the past week didn't help matters either.

"I can try."

Finn sat back on the bench, his arms folded across his chest. "I'm sorry you've got to deal with all of this. Can't be easy."

"It isn't. Times like this I wish...I wish Dad were around."

"I know. He always knew what to say and how to say it. Not my strength, I'm afraid." Finn gave her a good-natured smile. "And he always managed to find a way around every sticky situation."

"I don't know if he could find his way around this one. Over budget, under time. I've got people phoning me to book the place. I can't afford to turn away potential clients."

"But can you afford to disappoint them?"

Another sigh as the headache increased. "No. I know. It's just..."

"This was a dream of yours for so long." Finn chuckled. "I found that dream book lying all over the house."

"You and Reuben hid it on me more than once."

"Creating character."

"I've got more than enough of that thanks to you guys."

Carly slid over to the bid sheets she'd been considering and picked one up, frowning. No matter how often she punched the numbers in the calculator, how many times she tried to get creative with the financing, it never added up.

"Give Victor a call," Finn said, sliding out from the bench. "It can't hurt. Maybe the government has come up with some amazing new program for small businesses that are farm-based event centers in Millars Crossing."

"Not specific at all," Carly said with a quick smile.

Finn winked at her then left, carefully closing the door

behind him. The air conditioning kicked on, blowing the papers on the table. Carly gathered them up and set them under her empty coffee mug. She looked from her phone to the envelope Derek had dropped off. She knew she should just toss it aside, but curiosity got the better of her. She slid her finger under the glued-down flap, ripped it open, and pulled out the papers.

Her eyes skimmed over the introductory letter. So formal. Complete with letterhead and logo.

Crossing Construction had been in business for a few years. Derek bought it from a brother of his foster father.

Carly had been attracted to him from the first day he and his brother Kyle moved in with Thomas and Louise Kennerman as foster kids. He was exactly the kind of guy her brothers had always warned her against. Rough, gruff, and tough. But Carly saw something her brothers didn't. A caring and considerate heart beneath all the hardness.

Then when he was a sophomore in high school he noticed Carly, asked her out. They started dating, and he seemed to settle down. He started working, didn't party near as much. They got engaged. Made plans for their wedding. For his construction company and her event center. He would build it, and people would come. It was like a dream come true for Carly.

At that time, her uncle Gene, who was a Mountie, warned her that Derek was trouble. Told her that he'd caught him once with some dope, confiscated it, and let him off with a warning. But Carly didn't pay his warning any mind.

Until Derek got caught with cocaine and her uncle Gene arrested him.

Carly took a deep breath to relax. Struggled to shake off the old thoughts and anger, forcing herself to be dispassionate as she read through the papers. She had seen enough quotes that she knew what to look for. She frowned as she read and then came to the final figure.

Grabbing the other two quotes, she turned to the final page of them as well. Both of them were within a few hundred dollars of each other, which meant they were dead on with their numbers.

But the quote Derek had submitted was thousands under.

Enough under that if she accepted his bid, she would still be within her budget.

This couldn't be right. She pulled out her calculator and added up the numbers herself. And yes. The final figure and Derek's quote were correct.

She sat back, her mind racing, deciding. First thing she had to do was call the other contractors. See if they would lower their quote based on what Derek had submitted. Then the bank to see if she could get more money.

Anything to make sure she didn't have to work with Derek.

Didn't have to see him every day. Didn't have to see the painful reminder of who he really was and the trust he'd permanently shattered.

CHAPTER TWO

"*A*re you sure you can't get me more money?" Carly stood in the shell of her half-completed center, her voice echoing in the enclosed space.

"I've already put too much on the line to get you what I did." Victor Chernowsky, her accounts manager at the bank, sounded exasperated, and Carly couldn't blame him. Even before this she'd been nagging and cajoling, calling for updates and pushing for deadlines. Done everything short of baking him cookies. She knew a lot was out of his control, but she also knew that he would push if she did.

"So, that's a no?"

"I realize that's a foreign word to you, but you are correct. That's a no. Firm no. Absolute no."

"Got it." She tried not to sound as dejected as she felt, but it was hard. She was bruised from all the roadblocks she'd encountered. Bruised, but not out. Her stubborn Sutton nature wouldn't let her quit.

"I don't imagine there's anything else you can do."

"Remember that word you don't want to acknowledge? No?

14

Still no. Your only recourse is to get one of your contractors to change their bids."

Which she'd already tried, but they were even more adamant than Victor was.

"Okay. Thanks for all you've done, Victor. I know I'm hardly a model customer."

"Finish your center, start a decent cash flow, make your payments on time, and you'll be on my Christmas card list."

"That warms my heart." She said good-bye then slipped her phone in her pocket. The screen was still cracked from the last time she'd tossed it across her trailer in a fit of childish anger. That happened when the previous contractor bailed on her mid-project. Right now, she couldn't afford to replace it. So she had to restrain herself from physically expressing her anger. The cement floor of the building would be less forgiving than her trailer was.

She dragged her hands through her hair and pulled it back into a ponytail, looking around the building, forcing herself to imagine it complete. Brightly lit chandeliers hanging from the ceiling, windows framed with wide planks of wood, industrial tile resembling a hardwood floor. Tables graced with thick, heavy linens and decorated with lush groupings of flowers. Music playing from top-of-the-line speakers set discreetly in the walls.

A blink made the image disappear, and she saw what was in front of her. Exposed beams in the ceiling, bare walls, and a cement floor that was already cracking.

And now it looked like it wasn't getting finished unless she accepted Derek Gilbert's bid.

Her heart contracted at the thought. From day one she'd been hands-on with the project, knowing that was the only way it would get done the way she wanted. On budget and on time.

That wouldn't change with Derek doing the job. In fact, she

would have to be even more vigilant given how far behind she was on the project.

Don't panic, don't panic.

She hadn't seen him for over three years.

And for every day of the first two, she'd grappled with one version of anger and betrayal or another.

She looked around the building again, forcing herself to stay focused. This was her dream, and she wasn't going to let her feelings about her ex-con ex-fiancée impede that.

She walked over to the makeshift table that served as her desk in one corner of the building. Flipping through the binder she had put together, she found the contract Derek had submitted. With shaking hands, she pulled her phone out of her pocket. Her eyes flicked from the contract to her cracked screen, then back to the contract.

She had no choice.

She opened up her mail program and sent him a quick e-mail. Easier than calling.

Derek pulled up to the site of the building, and as Carly came out, he fought to contain the erratic beating of his heart.

She was even more beautiful than he remembered.

It was memories of her that both kept him sane and twisted his gut with remorse during those long, tedious days and long, noisy, and lonely nights in prison.

And now, after over three years apart, he would probably see her most every day.

This had to happen, he reminded himself as he pulled in a steadying breath, sent up a prayer for strength, and got out of the truck. Carly met him halfway.

"Thanks for coming today," Carly said, her tone brisk. Businesslike.

He could have come yesterday when she e-mailed but his own masculine pride kicked in. He didn't want to seem too eager even though this job, if they got it on budget and under schedule, could be the turning point for his company.

A lot was riding on it and he couldn't be distracted by Carly and memories of their previous relationship. That was gone. Like dust in the wind.

"No problem. I'm glad we got the job."

"It was pretty much a gimme given you were the lowest bidder," she returned. "Where do you want to start?"

"I'd like to see what the previous contractor laid out for a schedule. That's the one thing I didn't get from him. It would give me an idea of how his timeline meshes with mine."

"Do you have the sub-trades lined up?"

Kyle was still cajoling a plumber to come on board, they were working on the electrician, and Derek had a back-up plan should those not come through on time. However he didn't think he needed to talk to Carly about that yet.

"Yes. I do," he said. "I did some asking around and got a few who were supposed to work on this project previously."

"Good. That's good." She sounded surprised and impressed. Score one for him. "I was going to give you a list of who Alex worked with, but I guess you don't need it."

"I'll take that anyway," he said. "Wouldn't hurt in case we need to double up if time gets tight."

Carly held his gaze for a heartbeat then glanced away. That was all it took for his own errant heart to go double-time. He sucked in another breath and looked around the building.

"So, what's your take on what's here? I know you haven't seen it before."

Derek stifled his nervousness. Though he'd had endless conversations with one of the carpenters who'd worked with Alex Rotko and one of the guys who ran the pumper truck on this job, he knew his bid had the potential to be a shaky shot in the dark.

"I'll just have a look around, if you don't mind."

"I hardly can mind, seeing as how you'll be working here."

Derek nodded, still working around the surprise he'd felt when she sent him the very blunt and short e-mail telling him he was awarded the contract. He'd fought second thoughts, reminding himself of what lay on the line.

But as he walked around, making notes on his phone, the tension gripping his shoulders eased. "Regardless of his erratic work schedule, Alex made some good choices. I like that he went with concrete pre-cast walls. The concrete work on the floor looks good despite the cracks. The truss rafters are sound." He tapped in a few more notes, took a few pictures. Resisted the urge to snap one of Carly. A previous picture he'd taken of her had been a screensaver on his phone for so long he could almost count her hairs in the photo. When he got out of prison and got his phone back, it was still there when he charged it up.

He took the picture one afternoon when they went on a drive to the lookout point. She sat on the edge of the bluff, looking out over the river. He'd called her name, and she turned, smiling at him. Heart full of love. He'd proposed to her just a week previous.

After so many years of moving around from foster home to foster home, of feeling disposable, Derek felt that his heart had found a home.

Here with Carly.

He'd since replaced the photo with a generic one of trees and a creek. It had twisted his heart to see her face every time his phone lit up.

"When will you start?" she asked, her voice echoing in the distance between them.

She had stayed behind, watching him, her arms crossed over

her stomach in a protective gesture. He didn't blame her. He knew he had crushed her heart. Broken her.

He knew he didn't deserve to even be around her. As he glanced back at her, standing in the middle of the building, the sun broke through the clouds, shining through the open rafters, gilding her hair. He swallowed at the sight. Still so beautiful.

Please, Lord, he prayed, *help me keep my focus on this job.*

He dragged his gaze back to his phone. "I'd like to start tomorrow," he said. He knew that was rather ambitious, but the first part of the job was straightforward. Tin on the roof right away. Then set up the partitions for the rooms. Get the wiring finished. Something he could do himself in a pinch. Both his construction and his electrician's ticket were still valid.

Then insulation and vapor barrier.

"Okay. That's good...good to hear."

She didn't sound too excited. Derek knew they would have more of these awkward moments. Part of him wanted to rush over to her, catch her in his arms, apologize repeatedly.

He guessed it would be unwelcome. And he couldn't blame her.

"How early could I start without disturbing you or your family?"

"The center is far enough away from the ranch house so you won't be disturbing anyone there," Carly said, her arms still crossed.

"And you? Still an early riser?"

She narrowed her eyes, lifted her chin, and clenched her fists, making him regret the casual question. "That's none of your business and none of your concern anymore."

Another boundary he realized he had to keep in place.

"Sorry. I misspoke."

"You did. If we're going to be working together, I'd appreciate it if you keep any comments, any memory, anything from before...keep it to yourself."

She whirled around and stormed off, her hair streaming behind her like a warning flag.

Derek's sorrow blossomed in his chest, filling the space she once had as he watched her leave.

How could he have ever thought he could do this?

In prison he had created a fortress for his emotions. Kept them locked down tight. He couldn't afford to show any weakness there.

And he'd survived that.

He hoped those tools would come to his aid now.

That and many, many prayers.

CHAPTER THREE

*D*erek was running down the road away from her. Right toward a truck. He didn't seem to see it.

Her legs wouldn't work, she couldn't call out. She tried and tried to warn him, but he kept going.

What was he doing? Why couldn't he hear her? He was going to get killed. She tried one more time and all she could manage was a tiny squeak.

Which woke her up.

Carly sat up in bed, her heart pounding as the sound of a diesel truck gearing down broke into her confusion. *What's going on? What's happening?*

Tattered remnants of her dream still clung to her brain. The fear she felt as she watched Derek run to his certain death.

Her inability to stop him.

All emotions she had felt when she watched him leave the courtroom on his way to prison. She had tried to catch his eye. Tried to connect with him.

After he'd been charged with possession, he'd ignored her texts. Ghosted her.

She'd tried to talk to Kyle, but he ignored her too. Her uncle Gene wouldn't facilitate a meeting between her and Derek, because Derek said he didn't want to see her.

And the past few years, Kyle hadn't come to church and had laid low, so she didn't see much of him at all. The few glimpses she caught was the back of him as he walked away from her. So she stopped trying.

Carly dragged her hands over her face, blinking, trying to shake off the sleep that still dulled her brain.

She pushed the duvet aside then stumbled to the tiny bathroom at the bottom of the short flight of stairs of her fifth wheel. The cold water woke her up, but as she looked into the mirror she groaned. She looked like five miles of bad road. After a rainstorm.

Not good.

She needed coffee, and she needed to get her sluggish body moving.

And what in the world was a truck doing on the yard at this unearthly time?

As she got a pot of coffee going, she saw that it was already seven o'clock. Usually she got up at six, went for a run, showered, and was at work by this time.

Last night, however, sleep eluded her and Derek Gilbert was the main reason.

Knowing she would see him every day for the next five months didn't help either.

Finally, at two a.m., she'd caved, popped a sleeping pill, and dropped into fitful dreams.

She hated taking the little blue pills. After Derek broke off their engagement and went to jail, she took them every night for six months. Finally, tired of how groggy they made her feel, tired of feeling dependent on a drug, no matter how legal, she stopped taking them.

Until last night.

The truck was idling now and as the coffee burbled into the pot, she pulled one of the blinds, blinking against the bright sunshine pouring in.

A diesel pickup with a flat deck loaded with lumber was parked by the large opening at the front end of the center. The opening was eventually to be closed in with an entrance but, for now, was left unfinished so equipment and supplies could be brought more easily in and out.

Two men were unloading the lumber just as a second flat-deck truck pulled up and two more men got out. All wore hard hats and visi-vests.

Safety first, thought Carly, struggling to get her thoughts coherent.

And somehow her eyes immediately went to Derek. Not that he was too hard to find. He was the tallest, the broadest. His T-shirt strained against his biceps as he unloaded the wood.

Carly swallowed and dropped the blinds.

Get a grip, girl, or it will be a brutal project.

Three years ago, she would have been praying for strength. Would have clung to God's promises to help her through whatever she was dealing with.

But she'd turned her back on God the same way Derek had turned his back on her.

God was a major disappointment. She'd prayed when she lost her mother at age nine. Prayed when her father died just a few months before Derek was charged. But after that, she didn't trust God to be there for her. She was on her own.

Fifteen minutes later she was dressed, coffee in hand as she headed toward the trucks.

She was pleased to recognize Nathan and Pete. They had worked for the previous contractor. At least there would be some continuity to this project.

Pete looked up as she came closer, flashing her a grin. "Thought you got rid of me, did you?"

While Pete was a bit of a blowhard and big talker, he was also a good worker, so Carly was willing to overlook his more frustrating tendencies.

"Glad to see you back," she said, returning his smile.

"What about me? Glad to see me back too?" Nathan called out.

"Always, Nathan." The young man was tall, gangly, with a shock of bright red hair. There was hardly as much to him as the 2x4's he was unloading, but his narrow frame belied his surprising strength. Carly had seen him manhandle wheelbarrows full of heavy cement, push around screed boards and haul himself up, without fear, to the rafters above them.

"Nice to have work again. Glad I could see this project to the finish."

"I hope you're as enthusiastic when winter comes."

"We'll be inside then," Nathan said, still cheerful as can be.

Carly watched them working a moment, surprised they were doing everything by hand. She knew she had to trust Derek but at the same time that method seemed like a waste of time.

She stopped him when he came back.

"Are you unloading all your materials this way?" she demanded, reminding herself she had every right to ask.

Derek tugged on his leather gloves as he shook his head, avoiding her gaze. "I've got a forklift coming this afternoon, but I didn't want to wait for it."

"And what about the roof? It's only half done. You're not starting with that?"

"The materials for that will be coming soon, but this way we can get started right away."

"Okay. I was just wondering."

This time he looked directly at her. "I do have a plan. You'll have to trust me on that."

She wanted to make a retort about trusting before and look how that turned out. But she mentally shelved it, knowing it wouldn't solve anything to bring up the past.

"I'm glad to hear that, but you do realize I'm allowed to ask questions about the process."

He straightened, bristling at her comment. But then he nodded. "Of course you are. You're the boss." Then, without another word, he grabbed some lumber, hefted it up, and strode away.

She watched him go, frustrated with her reaction to him. Frustrated with his comments to her.

The steady beep of the forklift echoed in the building, and it was a wonderful sound. Though Derek knew the guys disliked manhandling the lumber this morning, at least they got started on the walls inside the building while they waited for the tin to show up. He hated having guys standing around while they waited for supplies.

He knew he was taking a chance, but the forecast was stable for the next week. Once the tin arrived, they could finish the roof.

He wasn't overly impressed with his foreman's attitude, but Pete Kolasa was a hard worker overall. He would just have to ignore the occasional pushback. The past three years had taught him a lot about standing up to more aggressive people. Standing his ground. He had the scars to prove it.

"What's next?" John pushed his hard hat back on his head.

Derek glanced over at the walls they had already put up, then back at the blueprint. "We need to set up some partitions in the room you just framed. Did you nail down all the bottom plates?"

John gave him a sheepish look, and Derek fought down a flicker of annoyance.

"Not all of them," John said. "Pete said we should get all the studs in place first."

"Yes, but the floor isn't completely level, so studs will shift around." Next on his list was having a chat with his foreman.

"And Carly was wondering if we're getting a garbage bin back."

He wasn't surprised that she hadn't spoken to him, but it still grated. Just a little. Would she use middlemen to communicate during the entire project?

"I'll talk to her myself," he said.

He made a few notes on the blueprint about some things they would have to change to make the work more efficient then, tucking his carpenter pencil behind his ear, he walked over to where Pete was working.

"Pete. Need to talk."

Pete frowned at him but shifted his tool belt and sauntered over. "Yeah?"

A little too cocky to suit him.

"First off, I told you to nail the bottom plates down before you put in the studs."

"But it's easier to do it my way."

"Not better."

"That's how I did it for Alex."

"Maybe, but last I checked, I'm the contractor on this job." He was worried about antagonizing his foreman, but he had to lay things out the right way immediately.

Start how you mean to go on.

His foster father's advice resonated as much now as it had in many other areas of his life.

26

Pete held his gaze as if ready to defy him, but Derek held his ground, keeping his frustration out of his expression.

"Okay. Got it." Pete gave in, looked away, and Derek felt as if he had won a small victory.

As he walked away, however, Derek caught Pete glance back at him, as if he couldn't believe what had just happened.

When Pete rejoined the crew he said in a loud enough voice to carry to Derek that they had to nail down the bottom plates with the cement gun. The annoyance in his voice wasn't hard to hear.

Derek ignored it for now. Though he knew he would have to keep his eye on Pete. Not the best situation. A foreman was supposed to make the contractor's job easier. Not harder. Once again, he missed his previous foreman, John Anderson, who'd retired a month ago.

Right now, he wanted to talk to Carly. Go over a few details of the blueprint that he didn't think would work.

Carly was busy in the old barn that had been moved and was now connected to the main center.

He pushed aside the plastic sheeting covering the small opening and stepped inside.

The whine of a belt sander filled the air.

Carly was bent over a large beam of wood, goggles covering her beautiful blue eyes, hair pulled back in a loose ponytail covered with a ball cap. Her gloved hands moved the sander back and forth, sawdust spitting out behind her, joining the dust on the wooden floor of the barn.

He waited, hoping she would see him. He didn't want to startle her. But she obviously didn't see him. Probably the goggles obstructed her vision. He stepped closer.

Her lips were set in a thin line, a frown wrinkling her smooth forehead, her shoulders hunched. She seemed upset and he had a pretty good idea his presence was the cause.

The thought bothered him, but he could hardly blame her.

He hadn't been in touch with her since he got arrested. Couldn't face her.

He cleared his throat and her head snapped up in surprise, her grip loosening on the sander. It spun away from her, shooting across the beam and landing on the floor.

He tugged on the cord to unplug it then picked it up.

Silence reigned.

"Sorry," he said, handing her the heavy sander. "I didn't mean to frighten you."

"Startled, more like. Sneaking up on me like that."

Definitely defensive.

"Again, my apologies. John told me you were wondering about a garbage bin?"

She tugged on her ball cap, avoiding his eyes. Again. "Yeah. Alex had one, and it was handy to toss the scraps in."

"I've got one on order. It was supposed to come today, but I just heard that it won't be here until Friday."

"That's two days away."

He knew that as much as she did but ignored her annoyance.

"I know. So for now, we're piling the scraps in one corner of the building and putting them in garbage bags."

"They'll rip."

"I've got contractor-weight bags."

"Are you sure they're strong enough?"

Again, he had to struggle to contain his reaction to her petulance.

"Yes."

She must have sensed his exasperation, because she lowered her shoulders and took a breath. "Sorry. I shouldn't be such a pain. Just under a lot of stress."

He understood stress better than she might realize.

"I'm sorry to hear that. I hope I can help ease some of it."

No sooner did the words leave his mouth than he realized

how they sounded. He was probably one of the reasons for her stress.

"I've got a decent crew," he continued. "I hope to hire two more guys once we start on the tin. Things will come together."

Carly fiddled with the sander's power switch. "I hope so. I've got a crazy long list of people who want to book this place."

"That's great. I think it'll be a fantastic venue once it's done." He should know. He'd spent a lot of hours looking over her dream book with all her plans for this place. Unless it had changed since he left, he knew exactly what she wanted this building to look like.

"I hope so."

She sounded dejected, which tugged at his already vulnerable heart. All day he'd seen her moving in and out of the barn. All day he'd tried not to track her movements. Keep his focus on the job. Sometimes it was easy, other times, not so much.

"It will be," he said, resisting the urge to reach out. Touch her. Reassure her. "You've done your homework. You have a plan and a strong vision. If anyone can make a go of this, you can."

She looked up at that, her annoyance seeming to fade away at his confidence in her. "Thanks for that."

Their eyes held for the briefest of seconds, and he felt a longing for time to slip backwards. For things to be different. For other choices.

She seemed to drift toward him. He didn't know if he imagined the faint lift of her hand towards him, but then she blinked and the moment was gone.

He swallowed then breathed deeply. Got himself back on track.

Stop imagining what's not there.

"Until the bin comes, just push your stuff into a corner here. I'll get my guys to clean it up," he said, his voice sounding brisker than he meant.

CAROLYNE AARSEN

"I can do it myself," she snapped.

There wasn't much he could say to that, so he nodded again, turned, and left.

The rest of the day slipped by but he didn't see Carly again, which was just as well. But regardless, he knew he had to find a way to deal with the emotions she created in him.

He had to put them aside. He'd had a chance with her, but he had obliterated it.

CHAPTER FOUR

A knock on the door made Carly look up from her computer then glance at the time on the top of the screen. Seven-thirty already?

She rubbed her eyes and shifted around the table to open the trailer door. Was it Derek again?

No. Thankfully it was her friend and future sister-in-law, Etta, carrying an insulated bag.

"Brought you supper," she said. "Adele figured you were still working, and I got caught up in my painting, so I thought I would take a break and join you."

"Thanks. That's great. What about Finn? Didn't you want to eat with him?"

"He's cooking for himself today."

"Cooking?"

"Cold cereal and pepperoni sticks," she said with a wry grin.

"Part of every well-balanced diet."

"A tiny part," Etta said. She stood by the table covered in papers and folders. "So, where should I put the stuff?"

"Sorry." Carly scooped everything up and deposited it on the bed.

"Aren't you worried about finding what you need again?" Etta asked as she put the plates on the table. She took a small salad out and a bottle of parmesan cheese.

"Nah. All I've been doing is shuffling them around, trying to feel like I'm busy."

"Things seem to be moving on the center at least." Etta tugged the foil off the plates, and the mouthwatering scents of spaghetti and meatballs filled the small space.

"Yeah. They got the tin finished by the end of the week and now they're finishing up the framing inside." She was still surprised at how quickly the crew worked.

Carly's stomach growled as she realized how hungry she was. Too caught up in her work.

"That smells amazing," she said as they both settled onto the U-shaped bench across from each other.

Etta smiled at her then lowered her head.

Of course. She wanted to pray a blessing over the meal. Carly followed suit, though she just kept her eyes on her food, unable to take part. Thankfully Etta's prayer was silent. After a suitable amount of time, Carly looked up only to catch Etta's knowing look.

"So, how's it going working with Derek? Is it getting any easier to have him around?" Though Etta had only moved here a few months ago, she was privy to all the family's past secrets and pain. Once they'd gotten to know each other better, Carly had told her most everything. Etta was a good listener. She understood the language of sorrow. She was well versed in it herself.

Carly gave Etta a vague smile. "Not really, but I'll get there."

"It's been almost a week. You should be getting used to him being around by now."

"Sort of. I just make sure I stay busy in the barn, and he seems to stay out of my way unless he needs more information. Mostly he seems to be able to figure it out." Her mind shifted back to the last time they'd been within a few feet of each other. How she'd had to fight the urge to move closer to him. Connect with him.

"That means you're not talking much to him," Etta said, sprinkling some parmesan cheese on her spaghetti.

"Not unless it's necessary."

"And how does that work?"

"Can you get the ketchup out of the fridge? It's closer to you than me."

"Ketchup on Adele's homemade spaghetti sauce is an abomination."

"But it's an abomination I love," Carly said, getting up from her spot to retrieve it herself.

"That's disgusting." Etta wrinkled her nose, telegraphing her opinion. "Besides, there're already tomatoes in the sauce."

"But does the sauce have..." Carly turned the bottle to check the ingredients, "Epices? Sucre Liquide?"

"You're reading the French part," Etta said with a laugh.

"Is there?" Carly demanded.

"Your ketchup schtick is a handy way to avoid my questions about Derek."

"I don't want to talk about him on my time off," Carly returned, popping open the ketchup bottle and squeezing a liberal amount over the noodles and meatballs.

"I can see that, but at the same time I sense you're angry with him. Might be better to let that out. Trust me, I know all about holding stuff in."

While Carly recognized Etta understood the necessity of releasing pent-up emotions, her friend wasn't around when Derek went to jail. Didn't know about the emotional tsunami that had washed over her.

The only one who did was Felicia, her solitary bridesmaid who had delayed her own plans to return to Detroit to assist in un-making the wedding plans. She'd protected Carly from well-meaning questions and encouraged her to hold her head up and not take the blame for what Derek had done.

But she eventually had to leave and go back to work, and Carly was alone again. Even her dear brothers, while sympathetic, were more inclined to beat Derek up rather than comfort Carly.

"I'm not sure I'm ready," she admitted. "And please don't tell me it's already been three years."

"I won't, because I understand. It took me years to accept my brother's death. I want you to realize I may not know what you went through, but I know that time doesn't always heal all wounds." Etta's quiet understanding easily splintered Carly's fragile armor. "And I'd like to think I'm a good listener."

Carly stabbed at her noodles, swirling them on her fork, suddenly not so hungry.

Etta just sat there, watching her, as if hoping she could get Carly to open up just by being silent, waiting.

It worked.

"You know what the hardest part is?" Carly finally admitted. "The fact that I never knew this about him. I never knew he was a drug dealer. I thought we shared everything." She huffed out a breath of anger and betrayal. "Of course, I can't imagine how that conversation would have come about. 'By the way, dear, I run a construction company with my brother, but I moonlight as a drug pusher'? Doubt the engagement would have even happened."

"Did you have any inkling? Any idea?"

"None. That's how completely he fooled me."

Etta took a forkful of her spaghetti, frowning as if thinking. "Do you believe that about him? That he's a drug dealer?"

"Well, I doubt he's doing it now."

"Do you truly think that's what he was then?"

Her question niggled open the mental box where Carly had stuffed all her second questions, her doubts, her anger and confusion. "The court seemed to think he was. And he admitted it."

"But do you believe it?"

She tried to keep the lid on, but a flicker of doubt winked back at her through a tiny crack.

"I don't know what to think. Uncle Gene caught him red-handed. And it wasn't the first time."

"Really? I thought he had a clean record before that."

"He did. My uncle busted up a party before Derek and I were dating. Caught him with some weed. Gave him a warning and let him off. I think Uncle Gene felt sorry for him. Derek and his brother had just moved to Millars Crossing and were staying at the Kennermans'. Foster kids."

"I didn't know that. Poor guys."

"Yeah. They'd had a tough life, but the Kennermans were good for them. Kyle had his troubles, and at first Derek kind of ran wild, but he settled down once we started dating. But him getting caught with weed was like years before he got charged with the cocaine."

"When did you start dating?"

Part of her didn't want to talk about Derek, but it had been so long since anyone asked any questions about him. Maybe it was because Etta hadn't witnessed Carly's emotional break-down, so she was less afraid to do so.

"I was in my last year of high school. He had graduated two years before and was working for a brother of Thomas Kennerman, who owned Crossing Construction."

"So how did you meet him?"

"He started attending youth group, and one night we got into a discussion about a passage in the Bible. When youth group was over, he asked me to stay behind. He wanted to find out more." Carly let herself go back to those heady years. The talks they had. They'd started out serious and soon became more personal.

And her love bloomed.

"So he'd turned his life around," Etta said, wiping her mouth with a cloth napkin she'd packed.

"Yes. He had. At least, I thought he had. There was a couple of his friends he would see from time to time I didn't care for. One of them, Tim, was rough and rude. He would tease me. Call me Saint Carly. The other friend was a fellow foster kid who lived at Kennermans'. I think Derek was hoping to convince them to change their ways. My brothers, of course, had warned me to be careful, but I told them they didn't know Derek like I did."

"Did he keep hanging out with these guys even when you were dating?"

"A bit, yeah. I kept hoping he would walk away from them, but I think he felt responsible for the one kid, especially. Jason."

"Did Jason do drugs?"

Carly blew out her breath in a huff. "Both Jason and Tim did, but not Derek. Or so he told me. And after we got engaged, I think Derek finally made a break with them. One of them had been working for him but quit. Derek seemed to give up on them and focused instead on building up the business."

Etta fiddled with her napkin, frowning. "So Derek got caught with this cocaine. Do you think maybe it was these friends that set him up?"

Again, Carly's heart did that little flip it always did when she thought of the possibility that Jason and Tim were the ones who planted the cocaine in Derek's truck out of revenge.

"That went through my head so many times. It was the tiny sliver of hope I clung to from the first time I heard Derek was arrested. But they had an alibi. Tim was supposedly in Lethbridge for the weekend. Three hours away. Jason said he was at a friend's house."

"You don't need to be around to plant drugs. They could

have done it and scooted off. Where did the police find the drugs?"

Carly held that question a moment. "In a toolbox."

"Which could have been planted any time."

Carly bit off the fragile hope that had taunted her as she went through every possibility. Every possible reason why this could have happened to the man she had given her heart and future to. "But he never claimed he was innocent. Didn't even try to fight the conviction. Just went along with everything. I begged him to tell me what happened, but he told my uncle he didn't want to see me anymore. Hardly the actions of an innocent man." Those last words came out in a torrent of bitterness that surprised even her.

"Do you think these guys had something on him?"

She held that thought a moment, turning it over in her head. "You know, I never even thought of that."

"It might be the only thing that makes sense. Maybe they got someone else to plant the drugs."

And once again hope seemed to rise up. Could it be? Could Derek have been blackmailed? Why had she never thought of that before?

"What could they have on him? And if they did, why didn't he confide in me? We were getting married. We always talked about how we wouldn't have secrets between us."

Etta crossed her arms, holding Carly's angry gaze, her own sympathetic. Understanding. "How did this all make you feel?"

"Rejected. Pushed aside. Ignored. Devastated." She wanted to stop, but having Derek around, even at a distance, slowly brought out the anger she thought she had dealt with.

"And I understand you had all the wedding plans to deal with."

"So many plans. Our wedding was three weeks away. I was so proud of the fact that the only last-minute thing I had to deal with was my hairdresser." Her voice faltered as she spoke, which, in turn, made her angry again. Finally, she pulled in a calming breath. "I'm sorry, Etta. This is so hard to talk about."

"I know. And I'm sorry if I've pushed you, but sometimes it helps to articulate what you feel. I know that painting, for me, was a way of expressing emotions I had bottled up, afraid to let them out because I had no one around to support me." Etta reached across the table and clasped Carly's hand in hers. "I'm here if you need to talk. I'm your friend and I want to be a support for you. I also want you to know I'll be praying for you."

Her sympathy combined with her touch and her caring was almost Carly's undoing. Her throat thickened, but she swallowed and swallowed. "Thanks for that," she whispered.

Etta gave her hand another squeeze then wiggled free of the bench. "I'll take the dishes back unless you want to finish yours later."

Carly looked at the plate of food she had barely touched. Her appetite had faded away during their conversation.

"No. I'm good." She got up to help Etta put the rest of the food in the container she'd brought.

As Etta closed the bag she smiled at Carly. "I know your faith in God has been shaky of late, and I understand. I went through the same thing when my brother died. But I want to assure you that God has not given up on you. He's always there, waiting. And He understands."

Part of her wanted Etta to stop talking about God. But the part of her that grew up with a simple trust in a Lord who promised to take care of her slid in behind her objections.

"Well, He might have to wait awhile. For now, I'm busy enough with what I've got on my plate."

"He's got all the time in the world," Etta teased.

Carly had to smile at that. "Anyway, I should finish up. I've got a bunch of e-mails to write and some more spreadsheets to put together before I can call it a night."

"Spreadsheets. Eeegh." Etta shuddered. "That sounds like my worst nightmare."

"Snowflake artist."

"Nerdy geek."

They chuckled and hugged, and Etta left.

Carly grabbed her papers off the bed and set them on the table, sorting through them. But even as her hands worked, her mind was busy.

Thinking about Derek's supposed friends. And what they might have had to do with his arrest.

But did she dare ask Derek?

"Once we get these walls up and finished, we'll have to get the electrician in," Pete said. "Do you have him lined up?"

"He can't come until Monday."

"That's five days away."

Derek shook his head. "I know. I can get the basics done for now. Drill the holes, pull the wire. He'll have to hook it up to the junction boxes and main panel."

"You can do that?" Pete sounded skeptical.

"I got my ticket, but I don't want the responsibility for the final connections."

"Wow. Look at you." Pete's tone seemed to suggest that he was surprised an ex-con had that much expertise. It grated, but Derek knew he'd have to learn to shrug those kinds of things off. He'd already run into his share of negativity.

Kyle had offered to move somewhere else, but Thomas and Louise Kennerman still lived in Millars Crossing, and they were the only family he and Kyle had. They had welcomed him back without reservation, which had made things easier. So had a few of his friends. However, there were people who gave him the side-eye when he was out in public. While he knew that would happen, it was still difficult to deal with.

"Yeah, look at me," he said, not smiling, holding Pete's eyes. He had to face Pete down and literally show him who was boss.

Pete seemed to get the hint and looked away.

"Also got to tell you that on Friday I'd like to leave a bit early," Pete said. My son is going to a basketball camp, and I'd like to take him."

"Of course," Derek said. "Thanks for letting me know."

Pete nodded, then left.

Derek watched him go and felt a prickle on his neck followed by a shiver. He'd often felt the same in prison, when he knew someone was watching him.

He turned and, sure enough, there stood Carly at the entrance to the barn, her arms pressed against her chest, looking at him.

When he came to work this morning, she was already busy wiping down the beams that she had been sanding all week. Hard at work. He said nothing to her, and she said nothing to him.

He thought he would get used to it. But even after a week of tiptoeing around each other, avoiding each other as much as possible, even the slightest glimpse of her still set his heart racing. Swallowing down his reaction, he reminded himself of what was at stake. He needed to get this job finished and on time.

"What's next, boss?" Nathan joined him.

Derek turned away from Carly, stifling a sigh. "What did Pete tell you?"

"To ask you."

"Okay. Let's check the blueprint. I can teach you how to look ahead." Though that was his and Pete's job, Derek had always tried to train everyone who worked with him to look ahead. Expect what was coming after so they could be more efficient. It was something he'd learned from his foster father's brother, his uncle, so-to-speak, who had taught him everything he knew about construction. Who had sold him the business.

He went over the plans with Nathan, pleased to see that the young man could think for himself.

Nathan strode off to frame the last room, Derek right behind him.

"Have you given any thought about hiring someone else?" Pete asked as he laid out the lumber. "We'll fall behind if we don't get someone soon."

"I know," Derek said. "I've been asking around and have a few ideas."

"As long as they can take a joke and put up with Pete, we should be okay," Mason, the other worker said with a grin.

Pete didn't look too impressed, but Derek just ignored him. If he wasn't such a hard and efficient worker, Derek might've considered getting rid of him.

He glanced over to where Carly stood, just in time to see her leaving the building, her jacket slung over her shoulder. He wondered where she was going, then realized it was none of his business or his concern.

CHAPTER FIVE

$\mathcal{C}$ arly strode out of the building, trying not to look at Derek.

For the past week, she'd wrestled every day between keeping her distance or marching over and grabbing him by the arm and spinning him around and demanding to know what had happened all those years ago.

But one question always stopped her.

Do I really want to know the truth?

This morning, after her talk with Etta last night, it had been especially difficult. She'd never thought that maybe Derek's friends might have set him up. Might be the reason he'd ended up with a stash of cocaine.

But why?

Did they hold something over him?

And if so, what?

The thoughts snaked around her mind and she struggled to keep them under control. Too many things to deal with right now.

Despite the work that loomed over her, she needed a break. She'd been working steadily ever since Derek came. Even on

Sundays, earning her a faint rebuke from big brother Wyatt. Though she didn't attend church often, she at least respected the day of rest she'd grown up observing.

Going out for a horseback ride would clear her mind. She strode into the tack shed, grabbed a halter, and looped it over her arm. Thankfully, the horses were in the close pasture and she easily caught Kramer, her favorite riding horse. As she led him to the gate, the other horses followed right behind. It took her some finagling to get Kramer out of the pasture without the others following, but they stayed behind. Last thing she needed was to have to gather up escaped horses.

A quick brush-down and he was ready for the blanket and saddle. She fell into a familiar rhythm. Settle the blanket, smooth it down, heave the saddle on, pull up the cinch, slide the leather strap through, tug down and tighten.

"Are you looking forward to this?" she asked Kramer as she worked. She always talked to the horse she was about to ride. It was a way of connecting, letting the horse know where she was and what she was doing. "Do you need to get out as much as I do? I know I've neglected you, but I've had things on my mind." She adjusted the saddle, pausing to stroke his neck. "It's been tough having Derek back. I thought I was done with being angry, but I'm not. If anything, it gets worse each time I see him." She stopped herself and glanced over her shoulder to make sure no one was eavesdropping. But the yard behind her was empty. She heard the laughter of the twins and Dean in the distance. Ruby Mulder, the nanny, must be playing with them outside.

The sound tugged at her heart. Had things gone the way she and Derek had planned, she would probably be expecting their child. Decorating a nursery.

"See, that's the trouble with him being back," she said to Kramer, laying her head against his neck as he shifted his weight. "All those plans and dreams..." Her voice faltered. Which immediately made her angry. After spending too many sleepless nights crying into her pillow, she had resolved he was never going to make her cry again.

And he won't now, she thought as she strode back to the tack shed.

She flipped through the bridles, found the one belonging to Kramer, then returned. He lowered his head for her as she slipped the bit into his mouth and eased the headstall over his ears, tucking the one in. "You're such a good horse," she said, stroking his head again when she was finished doing up the buckle.

She untied his halter and looped the rope around the saddle horn.

As she slipped her foot into the stirrup, she felt Kramer quiver, ready to go. But he stayed quiet, and she pulled in a quick breath, a sense of expectation coursing through her.

A few minutes later she was trotting off the yard. Kramer's muscles rippled beneath her legs. He tossed his head, but it seemed more in anticipation than protest.

With every step away from the ranch, Carly felt her tension ease.

It felt good to be away from the constant stress and tension of watching Derek every day. She felt as if things were coming to a breaking point with him. Not for the first time she wished someone else, anyone else, would have submitted a lower bid on the job. Or that she could've accepted one of the other bids.

But she had to admit that construction was moving along quicker than she expected. Derek knew what he was doing and kept his workers moving efficiently, which countered having him around so much.

She nudged Kramer into a canter and they went along the pasture up to the next gate, which she was able to open from the back of the horse. Finn had set that up because he always claimed he was too lazy to get off, unlatch the gate, walk the horse through, latch the gate, and get on again. As she rode, her mind ticked over her brothers, struggling again with the tiny nudges of jealousy she felt at the fact that they were settled down. Finding their paths.

You have your path, she reminded herself. *Your dream is becoming a reality, board by board.*

Then why didn't it feel like enough?

The dissatisfaction of the last three years rose up again. She had talked herself through these darker times. Found her own way through them. But somehow being back on the ranch, back around her brothers and her family, was a reminder of where she used to go for strength. For purpose.

Kramer seemed to catch her mood and tossed his head. Carly gave him the reins and he broke into a thundering gallop. The wind whistled past her ears, threatening to tug her hat off her head. She pulled it down, grinning with exhilaration as they raced over the field up the hill, down again into a valley and then along the creek. Finally she slowed Kramer to a trot, then a walk, and then made him stop. She walked him to the creek, and he put his head down, noisily sucking the water.

As he drank, Carly's eyes drifted over the view, and for a moment all she wanted to do was keep riding.

Ride away from her duties and responsibilities. From endless decisions and choices.

Sure, she was building her dream, but the closer it came to completion, the emptier it felt. And she knew all of it had to do with the man working on her center right now.

"We should get going," she said, giving the reins a gentle pressure.

Kramer gave in immediately, lifted his head, and off they went again.

As he walked down the well-trodden path, she remembered picnics with her family. Remembered her mother, who had died when she was nine. Those memories were less clear, but she remembered hugs and kisses. Remembered how her mother's voice rose and fell as she read bedtime stories. After she died, it seemed like the family became unmoored.

And when her father died, they all scattered.

Carly stopped on the rise, her hands resting on the horn of the saddle as she looked over the fields that rolled downward toward the ranch.

Her home now, and her future.

A few second thoughts and doubts assailed her. Was she wise to anchor herself so firmly to this place? Staying here, organizing milestone events for other people? Pouring her energy into making sure their dreams became as much a reality as she had hoped hers would? At one time she and Derek were supposed to have gotten married in a place exactly like she was building right now. They had gone over plans together.

Much as she hated to admit it, Derek was woven into her past as much as her brothers were. And now he was in her present, and it looked like he wasn't leaving Millars Crossing anytime soon. Her stomach twisted at the thought, and she realized she needed to make some kind of peace with him. To at least talk to him. Avoiding him had done nothing for her. Had only increased her awareness of him.

But not today, she thought. Tomorrow. She would talk to him tomorrow.

"You leaving already?" Kyle came into the kitchen as Derek was finishing off the last of his coffee.

Derek gave his brother a careful smile, trying not to let the rings under his brother's eyes concern him. The last couple of days, when Derek came home from work, Kyle was already in bed. And he rarely got up until Derek left in the morning. He got some work done during the day, so that was good.

"Yeah. I'm doing some of the wiring on Carly's center."

"You're that far already?"

"Yeah. I got a decent crew, though I'm going to need someone else soon. I've got a few feelers out." He didn't want to tell Kyle that most of those feelers were dead ends. It seemed there weren't many able-bodied men who wanted to work for him. He knew he'd been lucky getting the guys he did.

"I'm glad it's going good," Kyle said, walking carefully to the small table in the dining room. He eased himself down, wincing as he did so.

"Bad night?" Derek asked.

Kyle waggled his hand back and forth and, from the frown on his face, Derek knew he wouldn't get much more out of his brother.

"Speaking of wiring," Kyle said, "I got hold of the electrician like you asked. He said he could squeeze in a few hours tomorrow and Saturday morning."

"That's great. Thanks for doing that."

"Got to pull my weight somehow."

Weight that was slowly decreasing every day.

Derek suppressed his concern, knowing his brother wouldn't appreciate it.

"What else do you have planned for today?" Derek asked, forcing himself not to look at the clock. It was only five a.m. but he hoped to get a few hours of wiring in before the guys came.

"Thomas and Louise are picking me up this afternoon. Said they wanted a visit, so that will be nice. I asked if Alia could come, but they wanted to have me to themselves. I don't think they like Alia very much."

Kyle had only recently met a young woman he claimed he was dating. Derek wasn't sure how he felt about that, but Kyle was an adult. He just hoped that Kyle was upfront with her about what he was facing.

"Oh, and I almost forgot," Kyle said. "The company that's

47

putting in the flooring sent an e-mail. I printed it off. Just skimmed it."

He yawned, running his hand over the faint fuzz on his head as he walked over to the kitchen table piled with papers and books. He pushed a few papers aside, then pulled one out.

"Good news? Bad news?"

Kyle shook his head as he handed him the paper. "I don't know. They said they need to talk to you about the flooring before things go too far."

"We won't be ready for that for at least a month," Derek said, puzzled as he skimmed it.

He read the letter over, noted that it was dated over a week ago. Would have been helpful to get it on time, but he was neither in the mood to reprimand his brother nor did Kyle look like he could take it well. Especially considering he had contacted the electrician as Derek had asked.

Take the wins as they come, he reminded himself.

He folded the paper and shoved it in his back pocket. "Filed away for future reference," he told Kyle, making himself smile for his brother's benefit. "I'll contact them later today."

"Hope it goes good. Sorry I didn't get it to you sooner. I was tired, and you know things haven't been going good—"

Derek stopped him with a lift of his hand and shake of his head. "It's okay. Don't stress." It wasn't okay, and Kyle should stress. Derek gave him minimal responsibility, but he didn't want to get into that right now.

"Say hi to Thomas and Louise for me," Derek said. "Tell them I'll stop by again when I have a chance."

He'd only been there a handful of times since he'd been back. Seeing them for the first time after his release was so hard. They'd tried not to show their disappointment and, despite where he had come from, welcomed him back like the prodigal son. Unconditional love.

"Will do." Kyle yawned and ambled over to the coffeepot.

Derek didn't bother turning the radio on as he drove to the ranch. This time in his truck, by himself, was one of his few quiet times of the day.

The orange glow of the sun rimmed the horizon in the east, indigo remnants of the night fading in the west behind the jagged mountain peaks. He stepped out of the truck and took in a deep breath, enjoying this moment of quiet of praise to God for His creation. Every morning he allowed himself time to appreciate the open sky above him. The space around him.

He and Kyle lived in an apartment in town, and they could see the mountains from their balcony. But here, on the Sutton ranch, he could see them in all their glory. And every day he thanked the Lord not only for his job, but also for the chance to be outdoors like this. How often he had yearned for even a glimpse of the mountains during the years he was away. He had felt like he shrank a little more every day.

He shoved those memories down. That was gone. Past. He had a future now.

By September his crew would be arriving in the early dusk, but for now, even this late in August, the sun was slowly coming up already.

He was an hour early, but he didn't mind. The last few days he'd been coming earlier and earlier as Kyle slept in longer, a combination of pain and playing video games into the night to forget the pain. Somehow, he had found time to date a girl.

Derek fought down the usual sorrow at the thought of what lay ahead for Kyle. The last treatment had given them so much hope, but the past few days had been hard on his brother.

Derek watched a moment as the horizon lightened imperceptibly. With a faint smile, he pushed himself away from his truck and walked around to grab his tool belt. He liked coming early. Liked working in the quiet without the constant questions the crew threw at him. Pete did what he could, but ultimately the decisions were up to Derek. He was still waiting to

49

hear from a couple of guys he had contacted. He hoped he could find someone soon. Work was picking up and he needed more help.

He slipped past the makeshift door into the gloom of the building.

And the first thing he saw was Carly wielding a push broom, cleaning up the sawdust they had left behind yesterday. She was wearing earbuds, so he guessed she was listening to the country music she loved so much. Probably loud enough to deafen her.

His heart twisted at memories of them riding down the road together in his truck, music blasting out of the speakers. Every single time she would turn the volume up as far as it would go. If she was driving her truck, he would try to turn it down and get his hand swatted away. He'd accuse her of being bossy. She would tell him to grow up.

Simpler times, he thought, watching as she did a quick two-step, bobbing her head in time to the music.

This was the most relaxed he'd seen her since he started working.

He doubted she knew he was there.

Now the dilemma was how to approach her without startling her the same way he had when she was sanding the beams of the barn.

So he stayed quiet, waiting until she saw him.

It took a few minutes, but finally she did another dance move, spun the broom around, then looked up. Of course she jumped, but not as badly as if he had come directly up to her.

She yanked one earbud out of her ear, glaring at him.

The lightning change in her mood lodged like a cold stone in his gut. She'd been so happy for a few moments.

"What are you doing here?" she demanded.

"I work here," he said.

She blinked at that, lifting her chin in a gesture of defiance. "Right. Of course. I meant this early."

"Just need to organize before the guys come." He nodded at the pile of sawdust. "Thanks for cleaning up. Makes our job easier to work in a clean environment."

"Sure, gladly done." She seemed to relax at his show of appreciation.

"You're here early too," he said, trying to keep the conversation going. This was the first time they hadn't been either talking about plumbing, wiring, or preferences for how she wanted the drywall put up. Though those conversations were fairly quick and not very frequent.

"Couldn't sleep." She gave the pile of sawdust she'd gathered another push then twisted her hands on the broom, looking down.

"I got an e-mail a few days ago," he said fudging the time of receipt of said e-mail for Kyle's sake. "From the flooring company. They can't get the flooring you picked out anymore. Guess the company they were ordering it from went broke. So you'll have to get some new stuff."

Carly bit her lip, sighing. "Great. Just great."

"You didn't have a second choice in mind?"

"I'm not that confident in what to choose. Alex helped me pick out what I did. He had a better handle on what would work for a high-traffic area. More decisions to make." She rubbed her eyes. She looked tired.

"Have you had a lot to make?" He thought she had everything all figured out. He remembered her showing him her dream book with all the pictures she'd cut out and printed out. The Pinterest board where she'd put everything else.

"I've had to make a lot of changes to things I'd already decided on to meet the budget." She blew out her breath, shrugging. "So I guess it's just one more."

Derek pushed aside the work ahead of him. "I can come with you if you want when you go."

Her head came up at that and he caught the flash of relief.

CAROLYNE AARSEN

"Are you sure?"

He wasn't entirely. The trip meant four hours together in a vehicle. The thought both appealed and made him nervous, but he could tell she was stressed about this.

"I am. I need to get a few things anyhow in the next couple days. Kyle was going to put in an order for supplies, but the company said it would take a week to deliver. This way I can get it earlier." Which would save him some time.

"How is Kyle?"

This was only the second time she had asked him about his brother. The first time he sensed she was just trying to be polite, so he'd kept it short.

"He's doing okay." He wasn't sure how much information she wanted. He waited a beat and was about to move away when she spoke up.

"I saw him in town the other day," she continued. "He looks tired."

Derek stayed where he was, not sure how far to take the conversation. He still sensed a tension in her. He could hardly blame her. But he gave her comment the consideration she deserved.

"He is. This round of chemo threw him for a loop."

"I'm so sorry to hear that. It's been a tough few years for him. What with you..." Her voice faded away, and he guessed she meant to say "with you in jail."

"Yes. I wish I could have been there for him. But thankfully the Kennermans were here. And he was well enough to keep the construction business going, so that gave him some purpose."

"The Kennermans are good people," Carly said, lifting her chin to hold his gaze. "They were good for you. For you and your brother."

"I've always been thankful they took us in." He waited, wondering where she was headed, then decided to get right to the point. "So, what do you want from me, Carly? This is the longest conversation we've had since I started working here."

Carly's hands twisted the broom once more as she seemed to weigh what to say. "You know, when I went riding yesterday, I realized that neither of us are going away. You're rebuilding your company. I've got this event center. Until it's done, we'll be seeing each other regularly. Even after it's done, we'll see each other in town. I figure I may as well find some way to make peace between us."

Derek's thoughts seesawed between a soaring happiness and a cold reality.

She was simply stating the obvious and, he had to admit, she was right. They needed to bridge the awkwardness between them.

"I appreciate that." He waited though, the silence pulsing between them.

"So, yeah. I guess I just want..." She sighed, as if she wasn't sure where to go.

"You just want," he prompted.

"It doesn't matter."

"Actually, it does. If you want us to be more comfortable with each other, I'm open to whatever will make that happen."

She nodded, as if absorbing this, then she lifted her chin, her eyes holding his, her expression hard.

"I want to know if you've changed. If being in jail made a difference for you." She narrowed her eyes. "To use an old cliché, did it make you see the error of your ways?"

He returned her look, her words stinging. He knew he had to choose carefully what he said next. Not let her emotions wash over him and pull him along. Make him say the wrong thing. "I don't think you have to worry about me doing that again," was all he dared say. "But deep down, I'm the same guy you fell in—" He caught himself, knowing he had no right to bring that part of their past up.

"The same guy I fell in love with?" she asked, finishing off his sentence. "The same guy I was going to marry?"

For a moment he saw the pain underneath her bravado, still raw, still not healed. And it cut him to the core. The entire time they were dating, he struggled with the feeling that he was never good enough for her. He knew his past and knew what prospects he had. None. It was only thanks to working with Thomas's brother that he even got the start he did. Made him feel like he had something to offer her.

And right now, in many other ways, he had even less. Though he had pled guilty, wanting to keep things short and quick, lawyers' fees and fines still emptied the bank account he had so assiduously built up.

"I'm the same person I was three years ago." He held his head up, determined not to back down. Not to feel ashamed of who he was. He'd spent enough years of his life doing that.

"In other words, you haven't changed?"

He realized the trap he had set up for himself with his declaration.

"I've changed in the ways that matter," was all he could say.

She stared at him, her face flushed, her eyes bright. "That sounds really wonderful and I'm happy for your personal growth..." Her voice faded away and her hands clenched into fists at her side. "But after you were arrested...went to jail...I had...I had to cancel all those plans for our...our wedding." She bit the last word off like it was too painful to bear. "I had to cancel the caterer, the florist. The DJ. The tent company. I had to tell Wyatt he didn't need to walk me down the aisle. I had to deal with my brothers' anger. At least the brothers that were around. Finn was gone, Wyatt's wife had left him. Reuben had his own struggles. My bridesmaid and best friend left early." She stood there, her chest heaving with anger. "All of that. I had to deal with. Alone." She spat the last word out, and he flinched.

But what could he say in response to her painful truth?

Nothing.

"Aren't you even going to tell me why I had to do all that? What you...did was so bizarre. Something I never, ever would have thought you would do. What happened, Derek? What got you to that point? And why couldn't you share with me any of what you were dealing with?"

Her question rang out, echoing in the heavy silence.

Excuses, reasons, explanations, all crowded up his throat, wanting to be expressed.

But he had spent three years watching his back, keeping to himself. Three years and change keeping his secret.

And before that, years of caution. Of being careful. Of watching and waiting. Even with the Kennermans, even after he realized that what he thought was too good to be true, actually was true, he still walked around like he was waiting for the other shoe to drop.

Then, when he felt he could finally relax, when he met Carly and found his center, when he came to know the Lord and found a foundation, Kyle got cancer.

"You're hiding something, I know you are. What happened? Why did you do it?" She took one step closer, closing the distance between them. "What are you hiding?"

But he knew anything he said would not satisfy her.

One step closer and she was right up against him, her breath coming fast. She lifted her hands in clenched fists. Pounded them against his chest.

"What happened? Tell me! Why won't you talk to me? Do you know how hard this was for me?" Her voice broke and his heart along with it. He couldn't defend himself, couldn't say anything. "I couldn't even talk to you. No one would talk to me. Kyle wouldn't say anything to me. He just avoided me. No one would tell me."

He wanted to say he was sorry again, but how often could he repeat that before it became meaningless?

Her eyes shone, her mouth working against the sorrow he sensed she was fighting to keep down.

He knew he had no right to do anything. To offer her any comfort. But the sight of her tears unmanned him. He couldn't stand there and watch her deal with the pain he caused and do nothing.

He moved closer, resting his hand on her shoulder. It was just supposed to be a small gesture of comfort. But when she turned to him, his hand slipped down her arm, then across her narrow back. It was so easy, so natural.

A few shifts and she was in his arms, still suppressing the sorrow he knew was twisting her in knots.

He closed his eyes, fighting his desire for her. He had no right, but he kept her there, stroking her hair as her shoulders shook with suppressed grief.

"It's okay to cry," he whispered. "You have every right."

His words seemed to release something in her. She shuddered again, then again. And as her hands bunched up his shirt, her shoulders shook and the tears finally came. She released huge gulping sobs that shook her body as tears flowed.

Derek just held her through the storm.

Then the tension in her body eased away and her tears subsided.

His heart folded and he allowed himself this moment. Allowed himself to fill the emptiness of the past three years with the feel of her slender body in his arms, her head resting in the crook of his neck.

Her scent was familiar and created an ache in his heart for all they had missed.

He wanted to make it up to her, wanted to fix all that had gone wrong, but how?

He thought she would move out of his embrace, but instead her arms slipped around his waist as she clung to him.

"I missed you so much," she murmured, her words unexpected.

"I missed you too." This much was truer than he dared admit. He had tried not to think about her during those long nights in prison. Tried not to let his mind shift back to riding with her out into the foothills. Of their times together.

Of holding her like he was holding her now. Kissing her.

It was too hard, especially knowing he would probably never be with her again.

But sometimes it was his only comfort.

And now, he held her close, and all he could do was be thankful for this moment, however brief it might be.

She lifted her face to his, her eyes still bright with unshed tears. She gave him a wavering smile. "This wasn't supposed to happen," she whispered.

Then she released a heavy, heartfelt sigh and stepped away from him.

He was glad she did because he had come so close to kissing her.

Her throat worked as she swallowed.

He took a chance. "You want things to be easier between us and so do I. Can you ever forgive me? Forgive me for what I did?"

She closed her eyes, pressing her fingers against her forehead. "I guess that's one of the things I have to work through," she said.

Then she grabbed the broom that had fallen on the floor, turned her back to him, and returned to her cleaning.

He watched her a moment, knowing he couldn't expect anything more from her.

Knowing he didn't have the right.

CHAPTER SIX

*S*he shouldn't have done that. Shouldn't have given in.

Carly berated herself as she walked back to her trailer, trying to put some distance between her and Derek and what she had just done.

But even as she tried to be angry, she kept reliving the warmth of his arms and the hunger they awakened.

She swallowed down her reaction and yanked open the door of her trailer. She just needed a few moments alone and away from the project. A few moments to center herself and catch her breath.

And wonder how she was going to go forward. All she had wanted was for the awkwardness between them to go away. Instead, she might have made it worse. She had come way too close to kissing him.

Even as she reasoned with herself, another part of her mind said it was a matter of time. Despite all that happened, she was still attracted to him. Even though she didn't want to be.

She pulled in a sigh and walked into the bathroom. She needed a shower, then she needed to go over some of the e-mails she'd gotten. Then, once she got her emotions back under control, she could go out there and carry on. They were friends, that's all. And she had to put the past behind her.

It wouldn't be easy, but she also had to remind herself that they didn't have a future.

She just wished she could rid herself of the idea that Derek was lying to her. Holding something back. It shouldn't matter, but despite all her self-talk, it did.

Carly wasn't working in the building Friday morning. Which meant Derek had an extra coffee to drink. Yesterday, after she had cried in his arms, she had left the site. She didn't come back until later that morning and then she stayed busy in the old barn. He wanted to go talk to her but he didn't trust himself. Not after what had happened. So they both kept their distance.

The discussion that was supposed to ease away the discomfort and awkwardness between them had made it worse. He knew it wasn't the conversation that caused the problem. It was the hugs he gave her. How he had held her in his arms while she cried.

But this was a new day, a fresh start, so he had come early again this morning to work on the wiring. And he had brought a coffee for Carly, but she wasn't in the building.

He shook off his circling thoughts and forced himself to focus. He had gotten a bunch of wiring done, which meant they could start putting up the drywall.

"Who's that?" John asked as he parked the forklift.

Derek looked back, frowning as a faded blue truck, crusted with rust, pulled on the yard.

A short, wiry man stepped out and Derek's heart contracted. What was Jason doing here?

Derek strode over to the truck, shoving his phone in his back pocket. Trying to keep his temper down. He hadn't seen

Jason since before he was sentenced. The little sneak had kept a low profile.

"Hey, Derek," Jason said, lifting his hand in a casual wave. As if nothing had ever happened between them. As if everything was just fine. Derek was thankful that Carly was gone. All he wanted to do right now was grab Jason by the front of his shirt and drag him off the property. But he couldn't do that. He still had to report to the local RCMP detachment every week. All part of his early release plan. He clenched and unclenched his fists, and as he walked toward Jason he prayed for patience and for peace.

"What are you doing here?" Derek asked, struggling to keep his voice even. "What do you want?"

He must've looked and sounded more aggressive than he realized because Jason took a step back and lifted his hands up in a gesture of defense. "Whoa, Derek," he said. "Please. I get it. Don't be mad at me."

Derek released a harsh laugh. "Don't be mad at you? Why would I be mad at you?" Sarcasm dripped from his words.

Jason sagged against the truck, his usual bluster and swag leaving him, making him look deflated.

"I had nothing to do with it," he said. "Please, you gotta believe me."

"I don't."

Jason looked down, fiddling with a ring that graced his third finger. A wedding ring, it looked like.

"I know how it all looked," he said. "I know you must think I'm the worst person in the world. But I swear on my wife and my baby girl's life, that I had no part in it."

His expression was pleading now, and despite the anger that boiled beneath the surface, Derek felt a flicker of sympathy for the young man. He knew that Jason wasn't the brains of any operation his friend Tim had probably cooked up. Jason, like Derek, was a victim of the foster system. He'd been through more homes than Derek and Kyle had. And when they'd all ended up at the Kennermans', it had become a sanctuary for him as well.

Until Jason's old friend showed up in Millars Crossing. And things went south. Jason dropped out of high school, started working at the local feed mill.

And running around with Tim in his spare time. From the letters the Kennermans sent Derek in prison, he found out that Jason moved away after Derek was sentenced. They had heard nothing from him.

And here he was.

"You're married now?"

Jason's head bobbed up and down, still holding Derek's gaze. He raised an open palm. "I saw you in church. Didn't you see me?"

Derek frowned, trying to absorb this.

"Me, my wife, and little girl moved back to town two weeks ago. We visited the Kennermans. My wife, Julie, started going to this coffee break thing. Some kind of Bible study. Babysitting was free, which Julie thought was cool. 'Member how we used to always go to church with the Kennermans? I used to laugh about it, but not anymore. Sounds corny, but I've seen the light. I know I wasn't living a good life. Thomas told me you and Kyle are still running his brother's construction business. That you just took it over. I need a job. Want to support my wife and my little girl. I heard through the Millars Crossing messaging service you might be looking for someone."

Derek could only stare at him, still trying to sort through all he had just said. Trying to test his own reaction to him.

Did he believe him? Could he trust him?

"Can you give me a day to think about this?" he asked.

Jason nodded again, eagerly. "Of course. Of course, I get it. If you want, we can go to the cops. Do a check. I don't have any criminal record at all."

"Lucky you."

"You have to believe me. I didn't...I didn't want things to go down the way they did. I'm so sorry."

Derek gave him a tight nod, sympathy battling with all he had given up.

"I wish I could believe you," Derek said. He had so much more he wanted to say, but this wasn't the time or place. He was under a crushing deadline, with too much to do.

"Well, you know I'm a hard worker. We worked our butts off at Kennermans'. 'Member how he made us toss hay bales? How we had to milk cows by hand?"

This wasn't fair at all. This scrawny young guy was appealing to the few great memories Derek had growing up.

"Like I said, I'll think about it."

Then Jason looked past him.

Derek spun around, his heart sinking as he saw Carly astride a horse, riding toward the tack shed.

He knew the moment Carly saw Jason. She pulled her horse up so short he almost reared. Which was out of character for Carly. If anyone knew how to take care of a horse, it was her.

Derek turned his attention back to Jason. "Give me your number and I'll get a hold of you by tomorrow."

Jason nodded, his grateful smile cutting deep into Derek's soul. "Honestly, you won't regret this. I'll work my butt off for you. I'll do anything you want me to. I will, trust me."

Derek nodded, realizing that right about now, he wasn't sure if he dared trust him.

CHAPTER SEVEN

*O*f all the nerve.

Carly had to restrain herself from ripping the saddle off, tossing it aside, yanking the bridle out of the horse's mouth. She knew it was wrong to take her anger out on her horse. She took several calming breaths, fighting to gain control of her emotions as she loosened the cinch then pulled the saddle off.

What was that snake Jason doing here? Talking to Derek?

Her conversation with Etta the other day slipped back into her mind as she took the bridle off and led Kramer to the pasture.

She'd had her suspicions about Jason and couldn't dismiss the idea that he had something to do with Derek's conviction.

Her hands were shaking as she closed the gate.

She brought the saddle away, spread the blanket over the rail to dry, hung up the bridle and the halter, and took another moment before she gave in to her first impulse to go storming over there.

Please, Lord. The prayer was an unconscious, deep cry from her heart.

She tugged in a few more calming breaths and forced herself to walk slowly over to the building. The whine of skill saws and the table saw filled the air. Derek was walking back to the building, and Jason was driving away.

However, as if he had some sixth sense, Derek slowed, looked at her with a heart-stopping smile, and then strode across the yard toward her.

Another breath. Another reminder to stay calm.

"We need to talk," she said.

"Okay?"

He sounded uncertain but followed her as she walked a ways away from the building. Even though she doubted the guys could hear anything over the noise, she wanted to make sure they had some privacy.

She turned to face him, her arms crossed over her chest, her fingers tapping her arm. Restrained anger surging through her.

"Why was Jason here?"

Derek waited a moment, looking down at the ground. Then to her surprise, he looked up, his expression sympathetic. As if he understood her frustrated anger. Which only made her even more upset.

"He's asking for a job."

All Carly could do was gape, her mind whirling.

"Are. You. Kidding?" She left a beat between each word to emphasize what she was saying. "Are you freaking kidding me?"

Derek frowned. "I know you never cared for him. But he's married now. He's got a kid. He's turned his life around. He goes to church."

"I don't care if he had a Damascus moment," Carly said. "There is no way he's coming on this yard."

Again Derek looked surprised. Which annoyed her even more.

"I can't believe you're considering this," she continued. "Were you even going to consult me about it?"

"I would've mentioned it to you eventually," he said, straightening, lifting his chin. Derek never did like being challenged. But Carly didn't care. Despite what happened between them yesterday, she needed to have this out.

She tried to muster her arguments. But even as she was about to mention that Jason had probably been dealing in drugs, she realized the irony.

So had Derek.

"My reality is I need at least one extra man," he said, sounding reasonable. "And so far, Jason is the only one who's come forward. You may not like him, but he's a hard worker. And now that he's married and has a kid, he has a good incentive to keep his nose clean."

His defense of his foster brother was annoying and unsurprising at the same time. Derek had often talked about Kyle and Jason. How he'd had to stand up for them.

"I know how this looks," he said when Carly couldn't seem to find anything to say. "But I want to give him a chance."

"And what if he plants drugs on you again? Are you going to cover for him again?" The words burst out of her and she regretted speaking them the moment they left her lips. The moment she saw Derek pull away from her.

"You can't tell me that didn't happen," she pressed, feeling as if she'd just gained a small advantage. A tiny peek into his motivations.

"Carly, please, you can't keep doing this. What's done is done. I want to move on. I want to put all this behind me, like we talked about yesterday." His pleading tone surprised her and snuck past her defenses. "I just want to build up my business, keep my brother healthy, and get this center built for you. One foot in front of the other, one day at a time. Like my counselor told me."

His last sentence was a stark reminder of what he had dealt with. The fact that he'd spoken to a counselor, someone who was helping his transition from jail to normal life, seemed to bring the past he was trying to avoid back into the moment.

"Please, Carly. Just let it go. I'm trying to. It would make it easier if you could."

It's not fair, she thought. He'd moved closer, his voice lowered, intimate. Then, when he put his hand on her shoulder, it took every ounce of willpower not to move into his arms again. Not to seek the shelter of his strength.

"I don't know," was all she could say. "It's been such a part of me so long…" She let the sentence trail away, as if realizing that what she had gone through was a lot less difficult than his own three years.

But still.

She caught the glimpse of deep pain in his eyes before she turned away. And as she walked back to the barn where she was staining wood, she felt it delve into her soul and take root there.

Carly looked at the clock on the microwave, tapping her pencil on the papers in front of her.

Sunday. Church would start in less than an hour.

Ever since she had come back to Millars Crossing, she had been avoiding church and God.

Her anger with God over Derek and the loss of her plans and dreams had eased and been replaced by a yearning for the old relationship with the Lord. A relationship that had grounded her and given her purpose and meaning.

She set her pencil down and leaned back, her arms crossed, debating. She knew her brothers would be happy if she went. Etta would be thrilled. When Etta first came to the ranch, she had to move out of the house she was renting because of a fire, and one of the first things she had asked for was a Bible. Her friend's faith had been a reminder to Carly of what she was missing.

Her conversations with Derek had shifted things for her and evoked a restlessness she couldn't dismiss. The last thing she expected was that she would cry in his arms. That he would understand her pain.

Then, Friday, to see the pain in his eyes when he begged her to let go of the questions that haunted her...

He's a good man.

Words other people had told her when they found out she and Derek were engaged rose up. Reminders of who he used to be. He was trying to move on. Could she?

She shook her head, picked up her pencil, and tried to go over the numbers Derek had given her about the drywall and a quote she'd gotten from a couple of paint stores. She'd had to adjust her budget and, therefore, her choices.

But the numbers just danced in her vision and she couldn't focus.

Just go. What can it hurt?

From time to time she still battled the shame of the canceled wedding, but with some help from a counselor and friends, she'd worked through that. She could hold her head high knowing she had done nothing wrong.

But still...

She rubbed her eyes and looked at the clock again. She wasn't getting anything done. With a huff of annoyance, she slipped out of the bench and took the few steps across the trailer to the cupboard where her clothes were stored.

Twenty minutes later, her hair still damp but pulled up in a loose topknot, she was out the door and striding to her truck, as if outrunning the second thoughts she'd struggled with.

CHAPTER EIGHT

"*Y*ou sure you don't want to come along to church?" Derek asked Kyle, who was curled up on the couch, wrapped in a blanket. "There's a picnic afterward."

Kyle shrugged, his attention snagged by the television blaring from one corner of the apartment. "Nah. I don't think so. Alia said she was coming by today."

Derek walked over to the television and turned it down. "You're not too tired today?" he asked.

Kyle shrugged. "I slept okay last night, so that's good." He gave Derek a smile. "Alia won't stay long. Believe it or not, she just wants to play Call of Duty with me. Keep me company."

"You've been seeing more of Alia lately?"

Kyle nodded.

"Do you think she would come to church with you?"

Kyle pulled the blanket closer around himself. "Alia doesn't go. Her mom and dad don't go either, and I don't feel...I don't feel right about going."

"Why not?"

He shrugged. "Just don't."

Derek knew not to push the matter. Kyle had gone sporadically to church after Derek went to prison. The Kennermans, where he'd remained for the first year Derek was gone, would take him. But once Kyle was set up in his own apartment, he stopped attending.

"Okay. I'll see you later," Derek said, buttoning up his cuffs, wondering again if he should wear a tie. He hadn't before. It would seem a bit overkill if he did now.

The parking lot was half empty when he arrived at church. He preferred coming early so he could sit in the back. Just made it easier to slip in and out and avoid as many people as possible.

Thomas and Louise were already in their usual pew, second from the back, when he got to church, and he slipped in beside them.

Louise gave him a wide smile but looked past him as if checking.

"Kyle was too tired to come today," Derek said.

Thomas released a light huff of displeasure. "Wasn't too tired to be hanging around the bar last night," he grumped.

"And how would you know that?" Derek teased, knowing full well his teetotaling foster father would never, ever, darken the doorway of either of the bars in town.

"Saw him pull up when I was heading back home from a meeting at the Chamber of Commerce."

Derek didn't want to acknowledge that comment. He'd been struggling to motivate Kyle to take a more positive attitude toward life. To make good choices.

But how was he supposed to do that when Kyle kept telling him he wanted to make the most of the little time he had left?

"And how is work going?" Louise asked, putting her hand on her husband's arm as if to stop him from whatever he might say next.

"It's going well. We're on schedule. I have a few things to sort out." He'd been trying to talk to Carly about the e-mail from the flooring company, but she had been busy Friday and

Saturday, dealing with the company supplying the kitchen equipment.

He hadn't talked much to her since their embrace in the building on Thursday morning. And short conversation about Jason on Friday.

The rest of the day it had been difficult to keep his mind on his work. He kept looking for Carly, only to see her, at times, looking at him as she came and went.

Pete had teased him about losing focus, and after that he attempted to stay on task.

"That's good. I know lots of people are excited about the event center," Louise said. "I was even thinking it would be the perfect venue for your father's sixty-fifth birthday party."

"I told you. No party," Thomas grumbled. "Don't need to celebrate that."

"But just think of all the discounts you'll get," Derek teased. He was about to say something more when the sight of a slender figure moving down the aisle caught his attention.

And his heartbeat gathered speed.

Carly in church. He couldn't stop the lift it gave his soul. And the faint hope it nourished.

But then he caught Louise's curious gaze. He pulled the bulletin out of his pocket, unfolded it, and pretended to be fascinated by the order of worship, the announcements of various events.

But for the remainder of the service his gaze kept slipping to where Carly sat with her family.

"We forgive others as much to ease the burden on our own souls as to ease the burden on the person we need to forgive."

Carly sat in the pew, her arms folded, knowing how defensive she looked but unable to help it. The words of the pastor struck a little too close to home. Ever since her conversation with Derek on Friday, ever since he had asked so blatantly for her forgiveness, she didn't know where to put him in her life.

Whether she wanted to admit it or not, he was still so much a part of her. Even worse, even after everything that had happened, she was still attracted to him. Despite what he'd done, she could still see the things she loved about him. His kindness, his caring. His work ethic.

"Forgiveness eases the burden we carry," the pastor said. "Even if the person doesn't ask us, for our own sake, sometimes we just need to forgive."

It was like the pastor knew exactly what she needed to hear this first Sunday back in church.

It still felt strange to be here.

She had been angry with God so long, she wasn't sure how to let Him back into her life. But as she sat in church, she realized He had never really been gone. She'd just pushed Him into that same box she had pushed her memories of Derek. But God had been so much a part of her life that sitting here opening her mind to the songs and the Bible reading seemed to open a blossom that had been waiting for her to give it some attention.

The pastor announced the final song and as she stood to sing, her heart twisted. This was one of her father's favorite songs.

She couldn't sing past the thickness in her throat, but as she read the words on the screen at the front of the church, it was as if she felt her father's hand resting lightly on her shoulder. Reminding her of what she had been missing in her anger with God. Inviting her to let go of bitterness and anger.

"Come unto me, lay down your cross,
Come unto me, find what you've lost,
Leave yesterday behind, cling to hope that I give,
come to me, release pain and live."

It was an old song, and she remembered her father singing it while he worked. He had a deep voice and the song was like a blessing. The words were so familiar but now, she felt as if they were new. Fresh.

As the last words faded away, she felt the rest promised by the song seep into her soul.

Then, as she had a number of times during the service, her eyes slid sideways and back a couple of pews to where Derek sat with the Kennermans.

And each time, as if he sensed her looking at him, he turned his head just enough so their gazes snagged, then he would look away.

But this time his smile created a quiver deep inside her.

Leave yesterday behind.

Could she? Could she really let go of the pain and humiliation she'd clung to for more than three years?

And what good has that done you?

None, she realized. She'd been clinging to the pain, not the hope Christ offered her. Not to the freedom she'd receive if she forgave Derek.

Could it be that easy?

"Don't forget the church picnic after the service," the pastor announced, breaking into her spinning thoughts. "This event is one the women have been preparing for four months. Everyone is invited for a time of food, fellowship, and fun. Something I think we can do quite well here in Millars Crossing." The pastor looked around the congregation with a sense of expectation and excitement.

Then as the singing group in the front broke into the last song, he walked down the aisle, his Bible tucked under his arm, looking around and smiling at everyone he saw. He even caught Carly's attention and gave her a little wave, as if he knew exactly who she was and was glad to see her there.

She felt a hand on her shoulder before she left. "You're

coming to the picnic, right?" Finn asked when she turned to him.

Carly shrugged.

"Because if you go home, you're fending for yourself food-wise."

"As if I don't know how to do that."

"I'm sure you do with your two menu choices." He held up one finger. "Let's see, we have eggs." Then he held up another. "Or cold cereal. And if you're really getting fancy, both."

Carla gave him an elbow but chuckled at his assessment of her culinary skills. "You're probably right."

His eyes twinkled with humor. "Whereas here, you get a veritable cornucopia of foods. Not to mention desserts. Which I know are your favorite. I have it on good authority, there will be cheesecake. Adele's cheesecake." He poked a thumb over his shoulder toward Adele, who was chatting with Etta and the ladies in the pew in front of them.

Carly's breakfastless stomach rumbled at the thought.

"But you have to eat something healthy first," Finn warned her. "Be an example to the twins and Dean."

"Wyatt and Adele can do that."

Finn chuckled. Then his expression grew serious. "Glad to see you here."

Carly shrugged again, hoping she wouldn't get too emotional. "I missed this. And I thought it was time I showed up."

"I know Mom and Dad would approve," Finn said.

At that, she did get emotional. She swallowed. Gave him a wavering smile. "That song was Dad's favorite."

"I know." He grew serious as well.

"Do you miss him and Mom much?"

Finn nodded, his eyes holding hers. "Yeah. I do. You know, we're pretty lucky. We have each other. All of us back here on the ranch, I never thought that would happen."

Neither did Carly.

"And now you're back in church," he continued. "Things seem to be falling into a good place."

And just like that her thoughts shifted to how it felt to be in Derek's arms. How familiar it was. How comforting.

And how she yearned for things to be the way they were.

Which was foolish. That would never happen.

"Hey, dreamer," Finn said, giving her a nudge. "Time to get moving."

Carly pulled her attention back into the moment and stepped out into the aisle, blending in with the people who were moving outward. Chatter surrounded her, and laughter. She saw many familiar faces, heard many familiar voices. Some of the conversations were the same as always. How the crops were doing. Cow prices. Calf prices. Swimming lessons for kids.

A couple right behind her were discussing the sermon. She caught the sound of a child's laughter, another one's cry. *The ebb and flow of the community.* The community she would now be firmly entrenched in.

She followed the crowd out, most of them moving across the road to the school grounds where the picnic was taking place. Tents had already been set up and she caught the mouth-watering scent of hamburgers, hot dogs, and steaks cooking.

But as she walked, she kept looking around. Wondering if Derek was joining them.

And wondering why it mattered if he did.

"I can't believe he comes to church."

Frank Westerveld, an older man ahead of her, spoke quietly, but Carly heard every word.

Frank, wearing a very proper suit, white shirt cinched by a tightly knotted silk tie, and a disparaging expression, was glaring at Derek, who was a few steps ahead of them. A thrill shot through her at the sight but was just as quickly quenched by what Frank said.

"He served his time, Frank," the woman beside him said, her tone chiding.

Dot Westerveld was frowning at her brother-in-law.

"It doesn't matter," Frank grumbled. "What if he was going to sell those drugs to your grandchildren? Huh? You wouldn't be so forgiving then."

Carly tried to stifle the nervous flutter in her chest at Frank's condemnation. She wanted to grab him and tell him that they had just heard a sermon on forgiveness. Forgiving was exactly what they should be doing.

Frank raised his voice. "Well, I'm not impressed and aim to tell the pastor what I think."

Dot shook her head and then looked back and caught Carly looking directly at them.

She wasn't sure what expression her face held, but the woman grabbed Frank by the arm and hustled him away, her cheeks flaming.

Carly watched them go, wondering how many other people thought the same as Frank.

She had at one time.

CHAPTER NINE

*S*he was here, in church.

Derek still had a hard time absorbing it. Seeing Carly back in church filled the space in his soul. He knew his actions caused her to break away from her once-deeply entrenched faith. That knowledge created a ton of guilt he had to bury because he couldn't deal with it.

But seeing her back in church eased that knot in his soul.

And now she was standing in the dessert line. No one was on either side of her. She was all alone. He strode up to her, hoping he looked more casual than he felt. "What do you recommend?" he asked.

She jumped, her hand on her heart.

"I'm sorry, I didn't mean to startle you." Derek couldn't stop from resting his hand on her shoulder. *It was just to steady her*, he told himself. But he kept it there longer than necessary.

And the best part was, she didn't even move away. It was as if their moment on Thursday had slipped past both their defenses and put them in an old, familiar place.

"Well, I have to say I'm prejudiced," Carly said, her smile soft.

Relaxed. "I'm trying to decide between Adele's blueberry lemon cheesecake or her strawberry rhubarb cheesecake."

"Why not take one of each?"

She shot him a surprised frown. "That would be rude. I don't want to take a piece of cake away from someone else."

Derek chuckled, gesturing to the groaning table with the many dessert containers, some not even touched. "I think there's lots."

"You're probably right, but still..."

"But if you want to ease your guilt, I could take a piece of one, you could take a piece of the other, and we could just swap half."

"Just like we used to," she said, her voice soft.

She remembered.

"Yeah, just like we used to," he said, thinking back to those simpler times. Wondering, hoping...

Then Carly gave a firm shake of her head. "You eat way faster than me. I think I'm just going to take one of each and risk looking like a greedy little pig."

Derek laughed at that. "I don't think anyone could ever accuse you of being a greedy little pig. You've always had a generous heart."

She gave him a look. "Are you flattering me?"

"Always worth a try," he said, every casual word they shared making his heart grow lighter.

She chuckled, her expression questioning. "Didn't Kyle come with you today?"

"He stayed home. He was feeling pretty tired."

"The chemotherapy must be hard on him," she said.

Derek didn't want to talk about his brother, but sensed Carly's question for what it was. A gentle moving into other parts of his life. A return to some kind of relationship, however that might look.

He tried not to pin too much on it. She'd said herself she wanted things to be more comfortable between them.

He had to be careful not to expect too much.

"It is. It's disheartening. The last few rounds were hard on him, but he's beat some stiff odds."

Carly frowned. "What do you mean?"

He realized she didn't know. But if he told her everything, what conclusion would she draw?

"You know. It's brain cancer. It's serious, but he's...hanging in there." He faltered, hoping he didn't sound too unclear and yet give her enough information.

"I can only imagine how hard this has been on you. Especially..." She paused and looked away.

"Especially with me being out of his life for three years," he said, recognizing the need to be upfront about what happened. "And yeah, that was hard."

"But you're here now and working together. That's good."

"Yes. It is. But I have to confess I wish he was more interested in coming to church."

"We all have to find our own way," she said as she placed two pieces of cheesecake on her plate. "And I'm going to find my way to finish both of these," she said, deftly changing the topic, granting him a smile that was like a small gift.

"Commit to an action, then follow through," Derek said.

She chuckled. "You always said that."

"Got it from Thomas Kennerman. That was his mantra. Though some actions weren't always good ones to commit to." As he spoke the words he wondered if she would read a subtext in them but left it. No sense drawing more attention to the past than necessary.

He chose the strawberry rhubarb cheesecake and, without asking permission, followed her as she walked to an empty picnic bench in the shade of a poplar tree, and sat down across from her.

Carly took a bite of her blueberry lemon cheesecake, then closed her eyes in rapture, her hand on her chest. "This is amazing. The flavor. The creaminess."

"Oh rats, I didn't pick that one," Derek teased. While she was still waxing eloquent about the dessert, he snitched a forkful of her cheesecake.

She swatted ineffectually at his hand. Too late, he had already eaten it.

"No fair. You caught me while I was talking."

"Not too hard to do," he returned, grinning.

Conversation ebbed and flowed as people walked past them, some saying hi, some looking but then averting their gaze when their eyes connected, mouths turned down in disapproval.

Derek tried to take it in stride, but it still stung.

When Carly was done, she wiped her fingers with a napkin, set it on her plate, and put her fork on top. "That was delicious and worth every calorie."

She leaned her elbows on the table, looking at him, her expression growing serious.

"You look like you have some major pronouncement to make," he said, wiping his mouth.

She nodded.

"Perceptive as always. Yes, I have a confession to make," she said. "Something the pastor preached about this morning really stuck with me combined with something I overheard."

"What was that?"

She became quiet again, her fingernail tracing a heart carved in the wood of the picnic table, her head bent.

"You've apologized many times, and I heard the sincerity in your voice each time," she said finally. "I...I have to say, I wish you would tell me more of what happened. But I kept thinking about what you said on Friday. About sometimes we just need to put stuff in the past and move on." She paused, then leaned forward, resting her arms on the table. She looked up, her eyes delving into his. "When the pastor talked about forgiveness this morning, I had to think about you and how many times you've asked me to forgive you. I struggled a long time with what happened, and I still can't reconcile what happened with the man I know you are, but I have to believe that your apology is sincere. That you are truly sorry."

She pushed the plates between them aside, reached across the table, and wrapped her fingers around his hands, squeezing lightly. "I...I forgive you. I forgive you for what happened, and for what happened afterward. And for...for all the sorrow I felt." Her voice broke, and Derek's heart twisted. He had longed for this moment so much, but now that it was here, he felt undeserving.

You've got to tell her everything.

But he couldn't do it here. He couldn't do it now.

When?

He would find a time. Pray God would give him an opportunity.

"Carly, I can't tell you how much this means to me," he said.

"You look so serious," Carly said. "What's on your mind?"

He released another short laugh. "You need to know how much I care for you. You need to know how much it broke my heart, how it twisted my soul to walk away from you. To leave you hanging. I know what you had to do after I went to jail. We made all those plans together, and I knew you had to cancel them. I knew the humiliation you went through, and I don't know if I can ever make that up to you. Ever." He wanted to say more but had to be careful, afraid of what he might let slip.

"Probably not," she said, "But after hearing what the pastor said, I know I have to leave all that in the past. You paid for your mistake, you did your time." She pressed her lips together as if admitting that hurt her more than she wanted to admit. But then she tossed her hair back, shaking it off. "I want to move on."

He did too, more than anything. He hesitated, praying, wondering what the repercussions of telling her everything would be.

But right now, things were in a good place. He wanted to find his balance here, wanted to let the faint hope her words had ignited glow a little longer.

"I know it's more than I deserve, but I can't tell you how much I appreciate this. How thankful and humbled I am."

They sat there a moment, just being together. He wished they could go somewhere private. He wished he could hold her in his arms. Fill the emptiness that had gnawed at him the past few years.

Hope there might be a future for them.

One step at a time, he reminded himself.

Then Finn dropped on the bench beside Carly and she pulled her hands back.

He understood, but it still cut a bit.

Finn was grinning, his gaze flicking from Derek to Carly, speculation in his eyes. And behind that, Derek caught a hint of disapproval.

"So, which cheesecake did you like the best," Finn asked, jerking his chin toward Carly's empty plate.

She was looking neither at Finn nor him.

"I'm not going to tell you because you'll go right to Adele and tell her I didn't like whichever one I didn't pick," Carly said with a teasing tone.

"You know me too well," Finn said, looking disappointed. "What's on tap for the upcoming week at the center?"

"I have to go to Red Deer on Monday afternoon," Carly said, avoiding Finn's gaze. "Pick out some new flooring."

Derek noticed how she left him out. Which was fine. Finn hadn't come around the work site often, so they hadn't interacted much. But he guessed Finn wouldn't approve of Derek spending more time with Carly than necessary.

"On top of all the other decisions you've had to make?" Finn asked, sounding concerned.

"Well, I'll have help..." She let the sentence trail off, as if letting Finn draw whatever conclusion he would. And Finn seemed to come to the right conclusion, because he looked directly at Derek. "I guess that's good to know."

Right at that moment Derek's cell phone buzzed in his pocket. *Perfect excuse to leave*, he thought. He pulled it out of his pocket and glanced at the screen. Kyle.

"Sorry, I gotta take this." He gave them both a feeble smile then strode away, phone to his ear.

"What's up, bud?" he asked, trying to sound calm.

"I got bad news."

Derek's poor overworked heart jumped. "What do you mean? About you?"

"No. Not me. I got a call from Jason. He just told me he heard that Carly's uncle Gene is back in town."

Derek closed his eyes, resisting the urge to throw the phone across the grass. Resisting the urge to scream.

"That changes nothing," he finally said. "I wouldn't worry about it."

"Jason was freaked."

"He's jumpy."

"He told me he's working for you?"

"Yeah. I'm willing to give him a chance."

"I'm glad to hear that. He's a decent kid. Now that Tim is out of the picture, I think he'll be okay."

"I think so too. Are you okay?"

"Yeah. Just wanted to make sure you won't say anything to Carly, now that her uncle is back."

"What could I say that would make any difference?" Derek asked, once again fighting down his frustration with his brother.

"Nothing, I guess. Just glad you're doing the right thing. You're a good guy."

"Yeah. That's me," Derek said. "I'm the best."

Kyle was quiet for a moment, as if sensing Derek's annoyance.

"You are, you know. I hope Carly appreciates that."

Kyle hung up, leaving Derek to wonder why his brother had said that about his former fiancée.

"Wake up, sleepyhead."

Carly opened her eyes, trying to figure out where she was, disoriented and confused.

Her neck hurt and her mouth was dry.

She was in Derek's truck and he was in the driver's seat watching her. She sat up, wiping her mouth, looking around.

"Don't worry," Derek said, his hand resting on her shoulder. "You weren't drooling."

She gave him a feeble smile as she pulled her sleepy brain back to the moment. They were parked in front of an industrial-looking building. The flooring place, she realized.

Early this morning Derek picked her up, and they drove together to Red Deer. Carly had been alternately dreading and looking forward to the day.

But the sleepless nights caught up to her, and no sooner did they hit the highway than she tilted her seat back and fell fast asleep.

"Good to know," she said, blinking as she pulled in a long breath. "I can't believe I slept this long."

"I can't either," Derek said, smiling at her. "But it made the trip go faster for you."

"You should have woken me up," she protested.

"What? And have you fiddling with the radio? Blasting your

country music into my head? No thanks. The drive was quiet and relaxing."

Carly couldn't help smiling at what he said. His comments hearkened back to their past.

They created a tiny flicker of regret for lost time.

But yet they reminded her of what they'd had in common. Yesterday she had decided to move on and move past what had happened. She'd hoped doing so would ease the tension that hummed between them.

The problem was that, not only did it do that, it seemed to give space for the old emotions, attractions, and feelings to move in.

She held his gaze a moment longer than she should, then forced a laugh. "You used to hate it when I did that."

"I wasn't always as tolerant as I should have been."

His quiet comment made her realize he had changed in the intervening years. In ways she wasn't aware of.

"Neither was I," she admitted, remembering disagreements. Yes, even fights. But always, always making up.

"Different time," he said. He pulled the keys out of the ignition. "Should we go in and see what we can figure out?"

"I'm not looking forward to making more decisions," she admitted as she stepped out of the truck.

"What other decisions have you had to make?" Derek asked.

"After the other contractor left me in the lurch, I had to cancel a bunch of orders. Now, seeing how things are coming along, I've had to call them again and shift delivery dates around again."

"In a good way or bad way?" He paused in front of the building as he posed his question.

"In a good way. I have to say, I'm thrilled with the progress."

"Then I'm thrilled to know that."

She gave him a cautious smile and was pleased to see him

return it. She knew she had to be careful, but it felt good to be more relaxed around him.

They stepped inside the building. An older woman at the front desk looked up, her darkly penciled eyebrows pulled together, as if they had just intruded on her precious time.

"I'm Carly Sutton," Carly said. "I have an appointment with Nigel."

"Does he know?"

"I would hope so," Carly returned, trying not to feel a bit annoyed with the woman.

"I'll go get him," she said. She pushed her chair away and went through a nearby door.

"I'm thinking public relations isn't her strong suit," Derek mumbled as the door closed behind her.

"You think?" Carly chuckled, remembering how Derek used to joke about salesclerks, waiters, or waitresses if the service was sub-par.

Memories again.

The door opened and a large, heavyset man walked in, grinning at Carly. Obviously happier to see them than the receptionist.

"Hey, Carly. Glad you could make it." He glanced past her to where Derek stood.

"This is my contractor, Derek Gilbert. He'll be helping me today."

Nigel's smile slipped just a little. "Okay, then. Let's go see what we can do."

He opened the door again and stood aside to let them through. "I took the liberty of setting out a few other samples for your perusal," he said, sounding pleased with himself. "I tried to match what you chose before. I knew you'd want to replicate that decision."

Carly waited as he led the way, trying not to look at Derek, knowing he was probably smirking at Nigel's faint pomposity.

"Here's what I pulled out." Nigel led them through the warehouse to a pallet where he had laid out several samples.

Carly looked them over then glanced back at Derek. "What do you think?"

"Which color did you want?" Derek asked, lifting each piece, turning it over, bending it.

"I like the neutral gray/beige looking ones," she said.

"We like to call that greige," Nigel joked. "Get it? Gray? Beige? Put together makes greige."

"Yeah. We got it," Derek said with a smile.

"I'm thinking this might be a good choice," Carly said to Nigel.

"Yes. That's an excellent choice." Nigel turned to Derek. "What's your take?"

Derek set the sample down and lifted the one Carly chose.

"How much will this be?" Derek asked.

Nigel gave them a quote and Derek eased out a surprised whistle. "What kind of installation warranty comes with this flooring?" he asked.

"One year."

"That's it?"

"It's generous."

"You know this is a high-traffic building."

"That's a standard warranty."

"Not really."

Carly looked from Derek to Nigel, who wasn't smiling as broadly as he had before, surprised that Derek was pushing so hard. Realizing that she hadn't negotiated hard enough the first time around. Then annoyed that Derek was able to do this, but she hadn't.

"Tell you what," Derek said. "This looks like good quality flooring. I'm thinking you should have no problem standing behind it. You give us a three-year warranty on the installation and lifetime on the flooring, and we can talk."

"That wasn't the deal with the previous flooring," Nigel protested.

"No. It's not. But I've dealt with companies that will give out that kind of guarantee on a job this size."

Nigel adjusted his tie then eased out a sigh. "Okay. I need to talk to my boss. See what I can do."

Carly realized it was time she stepped in. Derek had talked long enough. She needed to show she was in charge. "Or you can bring your boss here and we can talk to him directly," she said. "Or her, if that's the case."

Nigel frowned, as if surprised she was finally speaking up.

"I don't know if that's necessary."

"Or you could let us know where he or she is and we can go over there ourselves."

Nigel pressed his lips together and gave a tight nod. "Fine. I'll get him."

Derek gave Carly a surprised look after Nigel walked away. "Well look at you getting all feisty and in charge."

"Couldn't let you run the show," she returned.

"No, and I'm sorry," he said with an apologetic smile. "I should have let you talk to him. I was just annoyed with how patronizing he was to you, and then I realized I was treating you about the same by taking over like that."

His attitude surprised her. When they'd planned their wedding there had been times he would interrupt when she was talking to a vendor. Often because the florist or the caterer or the printer would listen to his opinion when they wouldn't listen to hers. It annoyed her, but he seemed to get things done quicker. So she just gave in.

Guess his time in prison had changed a few more things in him.

"Thanks for that," she said. "Though I'm glad you pushed. I have a hard time doing that."

"You did okay for yourself." His hand brushed her shoulder.

Just a fleeting gesture that sent a shiver dancing down her spine. She wanted to catch his hand. Hold it. Maintain the connection.

"I had help." She gave him another smile, taking a step closer to him and brushing a tiny speck of sawdust that had lodged on his shirt. "We make a good team, I think."

"I think so," he said.

When she realized what she'd said, her heart contracted. She glanced back at the flooring, trying to center herself.

Their exchange seemed to hold a subtext she wasn't ready to acknowledge.

But it was one more thread binding them closer together.

She knew she should be careful, but deep down, she didn't want to be.

CHAPTER TEN

"*I* don't know about you, but I'm starving," Derek said when they finally left the flooring place. "Do you want to go for supper somewhere?"

Carly was quiet a moment, and he wondered if he had overplayed his hand.

He knew, back in the warehouse, they'd had a moment. One of the many they'd shared the past few days. He felt like they were both dancing around the edge of their feelings for each other. He didn't want to make the first move, but it had been so hard not to touch her. Not to want to connect with her.

And she hadn't turned him down. In fact, this time she'd instigated the connection.

"That's a great idea," she said, giving him a cautious smile.

A smile that held a hint of a promise?

He shook off the question, forcing himself not to read more into her actions than he should. Not to superimpose his own empty hope on her.

"I saw a place just off the highway that looks good," he said. "It's on the edge of town. We've been there before." The place was casual enough not to feel like he was trying to suggest anything. Just a quick bite to eat.

Carly chuckled as he opened the door to the truck for her. "So you can make a quick getaway?"

"You know me too well." He hated being in the city, or town for that matter. As a result, whenever they would go out to eat, he would find a place as close to the outskirts as possible.

He pulled into traffic, squinting against the lowering sun. The days were getting shorter, which meant fall was coming. Once the drywall was done, they would be finished inside for a couple of weeks while the tapers and painters worked.

"You look concerned," Carly said, touching his arm. Again, those tentative connections he wasn't sure how much to follow through on.

"Just thinking through everything that needs to get done yet." He hoped she wouldn't bring up Jason. He was starting tomorrow which, Derek hoped, would speed things along.

"Sounds like we'll do okay with the flooring now," she said.

"Thanks to you."

"And you. I always appreciated how you could be both forceful and charming when we were planning—" She halted and pulled her hand back.

"Planning our wedding?" he finished for her. "Yeah. Sometimes a little too forceful. I should have let you take the lead more."

"Which you did just now," she said. "And I appreciate that."

"I'm a work in progress, but I like to think I progress," he said, thankful for the quickstep over the conversational stumble.

She just smiled, and a few moments later he pulled up to the diner.

"I remember this place now," Carly said as she slung her purse over her arm. She got out of the truck before he could go around and open the door for her. She gave him a curious look.

"We came here after we went to talk to that company. About renting a wedding tent."

"Same place," he said, once again feeling another twinge of regret. One more thing she'd had to cancel.

"I like the food," was all she said. But this time he got to the door of the restaurant fast enough to open it for her.

They stepped inside. Country music played softly over the speakers. A young woman, the piercings in her nose, lip, and cheek glinting in the overhead lights, gave them a broad smile. "Two?" she asked.

Carly nodded, and the woman grabbed a couple of menus and led them to the far end of the restaurant to a secluded booth.

The same one they'd sat at before.

Derek stifled a sigh as he settled in across from Carly. He could tell by the way she was looking around that she had the same memory.

"I imagine we're going to bump up against old memories from time to time," he said. "I'm hoping they won't make you uncomfortable."

Carly shrugged. "I'm trying not to be. It's kind of silly, actually, but you're right. There will be a few awkward moments, but I'm thinking we're both mature enough to get past that."

"One would hope," he said, giving her a rueful smile.

"You know, I like your idea of dealing with things one step at a time, one day at a time. Why don't we agree to do that and not worry about stuff that comes up from before? It will, but I'm hoping each time it'll get easier to just acknowledge it and move on."

Derek held her earnest gaze, the vague tension that always seemed to grip him in her presence easing away.

"So, what are you going to have?" she asked, picking up the menu, obviously ready to do just that. Move on.

He scanned the items, then closed it.

"I'll tell you if you tell me."

She waved off his offer. "Nope. I don't want you copying me."

He chuckled, thankful on the one hand for her easy give-and-take and yet, despite his deep desire to move on as she had said, feeling a tiny niggle of regret that it seemed to be that easy for her.

The waitress came and Derek ordered a bacon-double-cheeseburger with onion rings. Carly got a clubhouse with sweet potato fries.

"I don't imagine you're going to share any of those with me," he said as the waitress took their menus.

"Your imagination serves you well," she quipped. "You know I'm not so generous with sweet potato fries."

"Unless I steal one."

"And find out how it feels to get your fingers rapped with a fork."

"I wouldn't be dumb enough to use my fingers," he returned, a small bubble of happy contentment rising up. He knew he shouldn't allow it any space, but the loneliness that at times had teeth still surrounded him. The ache he felt for what he'd lost.

"Oh, I got a text last night," Carly said, turning businesslike. "I've been talking to the company installing the sound system. They were wondering if they could come and have a look at the place at this stage."

"Sure. I don't know what they hope to figure out."

"They said they want to consult with the electrician."

Derek nodded, understanding that. He asked her a few more questions, and they easily slipped back into talk about the center.

When the waitress delivered their food, she gave them both a bright smile. "Enjoy," she said, but she didn't leave right away. Derek looked up at her to see what she wanted. "I hope I'm not being nosy, but I think I remember you guys. It was a long time ago, but you came in here a couple of times. I had just started, and you gave me a big tip." She looked at Derek. "You were planning your wedding. I remember that because I was too. I couldn't help listening to what you guys were talking about. You had such cool ideas. How was the wedding?"

Derek felt his heart freeze. He blinked as he struggled to grab a coherent thought. "Well, there was...something happened—"

"We called the wedding off," Carly said, smiling at the waitress. "It was hard but needed to be done."

The waitress's mouth fell open in shocked embarrassment and her cheeks flamed red. "I'm so sorry. I didn't realize. I feel so stupid."

"It's fine," Carly said. "How were you to know? Anyway, that's in the past, and now we're working together so..." She shrugged, letting the waitress draw her own conclusion from the unfinished sentence.

"I'm sorry. Again. Please forgive me."

"There's nothing to forgive," Derek said. "Like Carly said, you didn't know."

"I'm not usually so nosy, but you know, you guys seemed so in love." She closed her eyes, smacking the palm of her hand on her forehead. "Never mind. I'm out of here."

Derek watched her hurry away, feeling sorry for her.

"Poor girl," Carly said. "Talk about putting your foot in it."

"No kidding." Derek was pleased to hear how casual Carly was about it all. "Anyway, my stomach is growling." He folded his hands on the table then, with a quick glance at Carly, lowered his head. He sent up a silent prayer for a blessing on the food, for moments of peace with Carly, and for wisdom going forward. And, at the end, he sent up yet another prayer for his brother. For peace and for strength.

He lifted his head and caught Carly looking at him. "Your

faith seems to have deepened," she said, "even despite...well, time in prison."

"That's what helped me through," he said. "Knowing that the Lord was watching over me and that whatever happened I'd receive strength to endure it."

He caught himself, hoping he wasn't laying it on too thick.

"Did you have to endure a lot?" she asked.

Okay, we're doing this, he thought.

Though he wanted to move forward, his three years in prison had been a part of his life he couldn't ignore or forget. Carly had made many sacrifices. He at least owed her some glimpse into his life after they had broken up.

"It was hard. But I was lucky. I'm a decent-sized guy. In good shape, so it was harder to intimidate me. Especially when I got a new cellmate. He was even bigger than me and a stronger Christian than me. We looked out for each other and prayed for each other."

"Where is he now?"

"He's still there. Won't get out for another five years, if he's lucky. He was in for attempted murder. Some guy was beating up on his sister. He wanted to take care of her. I could identify. Not that I had a sister or anything, but the idea of taking care of your family. We connected on that level as well." He caught himself, hoping she wouldn't catch the slip.

"And he was a Christian?"

"Not when he got in. But he found a Bible study group and started going before he was transferred to where I was." He gave her a careful smile and took a huge leap of faith and trust. "And what about you? What kept you busy while I was incarcerated?" He took a bite of his burger, hoping she would get the hint. His time in prison was something he really preferred not to talk about.

Carly dipped her fry into the small bowl of chipotle sauce, wrinkling her forehead as if thinking. "I left after I canceled all the wedding stuff. Moved to Yellowknife. Got a job working there for a guide-outfitter. I helped wrangle the horses." She popped the fry in her mouth and grinned. "Same stuff I was doing here. Did that for the rest of the summer then took a trip to Australia. Worked for a firefighting crew for a season. Then came back and lived in Calgary for a bit, and worked for a wedding consultant. She was the one who pushed me to get my event center going. Told me she could get me clients if I did. And she was right. I was surprised at how many people were willing to consider booking their event this far out of town. When I initially planned this place, I thought I'd have to buy land closer to Calgary."

"And you have lots of bookings?" he asked, preferring not to think of Carly wandering the world, doing whatever came to mind. She'd always been so single-minded. So focused.

"I do." She gave him a tight smile. "If I can get it finished on time."

Derek wanted to give her instant reassurance but knew better. He'd been in the construction business long enough not to make empty promises and to know that there were too many variables to guarantee a precise end date. Even though he had a good idea he would be done close to on-time, other people would be coming in behind him that he didn't have as much control over.

"We'll do our best to make that happen," he said, giving her what he hoped was a reassuring smile. He took another bite of his hamburger, appreciating the smoky, juicy flavor.

"I'm already feeling a lot better than I was a few weeks ago," Carly said. She leaned forward, eyeing his plate. "You've got a lot of onion rings there, don't you?"

"Yes. I do. And I'm going to take the high road and offer you some."

Carly chuckled, then swapped some of his onion rings for some of her sweet potato fries. "You're an inspiration to me."

He wished that were true in other areas, but for now, with her smiling at him, with things seeming to settle into a better routine, he was content.

They chatted as they ate, falling into an easy rhythm. *It was never hard with her*, Derek thought with a flicker of nostalgia.

Three-quarters of an hour later they were back in his truck and back on the road.

Carly fell asleep again, and Derek smiled at the sight. She always had a hard time staying awake on long trips.

By the time they pulled onto the ranch the sun was flirting with the horizon. He drove up to her trailer and parked beside her truck. He left the engine running and just watched her, giving himself the luxury of letting his eyes wander over her beloved face.

He knew he was playing a dangerous game, but it had been so long. And he just wanted to look at her.

But she must have sensed him staring at her. She blinked, turned her head toward him and then, to his surprise, gave him a soft, warm smile.

"Hey, you," she said, her voice husky, like it always was when she woke up after a nap in the vehicle. She stretched her arms out, turned her head to work out a kink in her neck, then breathed in deeply. "Sorry about that," she said, then chuckled. "Actually, that's a lie. I'm not sorry at all."

"Obviously you needed the sleep." He shifted his arm, wishing the truck didn't have that dumb console between them. He could flip it up, but that would be far too obvious. Too strong a move.

"I did. Haven't been sleeping that well," she admitted.

"Sorry to hear that. Stress?"

She was quiet a moment. "That and other things."

She sounded so serious. He would have liked to ask but sensed he might not like what she would say. They were still tiptoeing their way around each other. Still not sure how optimistic he was allowed to be.

"When does Jason start?" she asked.

"Tomorrow."

She nodded. "Okay. Good to know."

"He's a good kid," Derek said, feeling a sudden need to defend Jason. "He's really trying to turn his life around."

"I know. I think that's good, and I'm glad to hear it."

Then, to his shock and surprise, she brushed her hand over his forearm. Her touch was featherlight, but he felt like an electric shock ran up his arm. He wanted to catch her hand in his, but figured he better play it safe. Be careful.

If things were going the way he thought, they had time.

"Mmm, this is great coffee." Carly rested her feet on the crossbeam of the sawhorse Derek had pulled over and took another sip, then eased out a grateful sigh.

"Creamy and sweet. Just the way you like it."

"You know me too well." She took another sip, looking around the interior of the building that had taken up so much of her mental space. "Tapers are coming end of the week?" she asked.

She knew, but right now it was quiet in the building. Derek's crew wouldn't be coming for at least another hour. She just wanted to make easy conversation.

Yesterday she had come early with the faint hope that Derek would be there, but he didn't come until after the crew did. This morning, however, he was there, waiting with an insulated mug of coffee for her and one for himself.

Crazy how happy that made her.

"Yep. They'll be busy a few days. Thankfully the rain has held off, which means we can work outside on the patio."

"I'm excited to see what the concrete will look like."

"I'm confident you'll like the stamped look. Cheaper than the aggregate you initially hoped for and easier to maintain."

"So you told me." She smiled at him, their eyes holding a little longer than necessary.

That had been happening more and more. Every time she came into the center, it was as if they looked for each other. Found each other. Exchanged a look, a smile. A connection.

She couldn't ignore or pass off anymore what was happening. Still holding his steady gaze, she took another sip of her coffee then put the mug down. She was tired of dreaming about him. Tired of this back-and-forth.

At one time they had loved each other. At one time they were going to spend their lives together.

He had made a huge mistake. Had paid for it. He wanted to move on and she had forgiven him.

She had missed him so much. Still missed him in many ways.

The past week she'd sensed the old connection growing. The times their eyes would meet. The gentle smiles they exchanged.

They'd had something before, and it was coming back fourfold. She was tired of dissembling.

So she walked over to him, took his coffee mug out of his hand, set it aside, then stepped into his arms, slipping her own around him.

Derek kept some distance between them, leaning back to look into her eyes, his hands resting on her hips. "What are you doing, Carly?"

"Giving in," was all she could say. "I'm tired of pretending that what we once had isn't coming back."

He swallowed hard, and his hands tightened as he dragged in a breath. "Are you sure?"

"No. I'm not. But I missed you and I know you missed me. I told you, I've forgiven you and I know you've changed. I have to believe that. I want to believe that. Because I'm tired of ignoring what's growing between us."

Derek laid his forehead against hers, and his face grew blurry. "Please be sure of what you're starting here," he said. "I'm asking you, for my sake, don't do this just because something is missing in your life."

The uncertain pain in his voice cut through her. However, she was also thankful for his speaking the truth, hard as it was to hear.

"Something is missing from my life. You. But I'm not just toying with you. I wouldn't do that. Couldn't." She wanted to sound confident, but her trembling voice gave away her emotions.

She laid her head against his shoulder, willing her whirling thoughts to slow. To go away. "I've missed you so much and I know that what we had was important."

Then she felt Derek's fingers slipping through her hair. Felt him twirl a lock of it around his finger. The gesture resurrected old memories, better memories. Times they would sit together on a blanket, leaning against a tree, at the lookout point on the river. Talking about their future. "I need to know if you can put what I did behind you," he said.

"It'll be hard," Carly admitted. "You just came back into my life. I've struggled with what you did. But knowing that you're not that guy, knowing that you want to move past that... That all helps."

"I know being with an ex-con won't be easy, but I want you to believe that I will do anything to make that right. I need you to believe that."

"I do," Carly said, straightening again, slipping her hand around his neck, tangling her fingers in his hair that had grown longer since he started the job. Her old Derek. "You're a good man and I know that." As she spoke the words they settled in her soul. Became a part of her.

And they gently pried up old memories.

How respectful Derek was when he first met her brothers. How he had accepted their warnings to be careful with their sister's heart.

How quiet he could be when other people were talking. Despite his rough past, he didn't need to draw attention to himself. It was what drew her to him in the first place. After being around three brothers who either ignored or teased her mercilessly, to be with someone who listened intently to her was novel and gratifying.

"You didn't need to change that much," she admitted. "You were always a good person. And you still are."

"Just because I go to church..." He gave her a crooked smile which did nothing for her equilibrium.

She nestled against him, allowing herself to shift away the memories of the last few years. She fought down a flicker of guilt, that she was giving in too easily. But being with him the last few weeks, watching him with his crew, with his brother, with the people in the church, showed her what a good man he truly was. She knew that deep in her soul.

"I don't think I've ever stopped loving you," she admitted.

His arms tightened around her, pulling her even closer as he rested his head on hers.

"I don't deserve that," he said. "I can't tell you how grateful that makes me feel. How undeserving. I know leaving you hanging just before our wedding, being in jail, will be hard things to overcome, but I feel in my heart..." He let his sentence trail off. She lifted her head to look at him, frowning.

"You feel in your heart what?"

He caught her face between his large work-roughened hands, thumbs stroking her cheeks, his eyes delving into hers. "I know in my heart we were meant for each other. I don't deserve you at all—"

She pressed her finger to his lips, stopping his admission.

"We don't need to talk about deserving or not deserving. None of us deserve any of the things we have. I don't deserve to have the support I do from my brothers. I don't deserve to have the community I live in. The life I lead. I know I've been blessed and fortunate. And I know you haven't. So let's not talk about who deserves what."

His hands relaxed a little and his shoulders relaxed, as if releasing a burden he had been carrying.

"I wish I could tell you how much you mean to me. Wish I could tell you how much I love you. Words are too small."

"Well then, show me," she taunted.

He needed no further encouragement. His mouth lowered to hers, their lips met, and Carly sank into his embrace.

This was right, this was where she belonged. Their mouths were hungry, almost devouring each other, trying to make up for lost time. He held her so close she thought she might run out of breath, but his kisses made her more breathless than his embrace did.

"Carly," he whispered against her mouth, "I missed you so much." He rained kisses all over her face then came back to her mouth, his lips hungrily seeking. Their kiss deepened, and Carly felt as if she had come home.

CHAPTER ELEVEN

"*D*o you need us to do anything in here?" Derek asked, pushing aside the plastic strips that separated the barn from the rest of the building.

Carly looked up from the endless rows of beams she was staining. Though she wore a face mask today, it wasn't hard to see the smile that crinkled her eyes. She set the brush aside, pulled off her rubber gloves and facemask, and set them aside. "I don't need your crew to do anything, but I do need something from you."

She walked over to him, pulled him away from the entrance, wrapped her arms around him, and kissed him soundly.

"Been wanting to do that all day," she said, her hands linked behind his neck. She leaned back to look up at him.

"I have too," he said, his heart full and yet light. He was still absorbing the reality of Carly back in his life, back in his arms. Yesterday still seemed surreal. Too good to be true. "In fact, that was one reason I figured I'd come in and make an offer I knew you couldn't say no to."

"Empty promises." She shook her head in mock dismay.

"Not at all. If you needed any help, you know I would offer it."

She was quiet a moment, her eyes shifting to the top button of his shirt. Her expression grew serious. "So, how is Jason working out for you?"

A thread of anxiety tightened around his heart. He wondered where she was going with this but decided to play it at face value.

"Well, he just started today, so it's early to make a full judgment, but he's good. Knows his stuff. He used to work for my uncle, you know."

"I do know," Carly said. She still kept her eyes away from his. "I'm glad it's working out."

"It's made a big difference. Taken some of the weight off me."

"That why you weren't in early this morning?" she teased, now lifting her gaze to his.

"No. I like our early morning coffee time. Kyle needed some help with a few things he's working on."

That was partly the truth. The other was that his brother also spent most of the night in the bathroom, vomiting. When he finally got to sleep, it was after four. As a result, Derek was so tired he slept through his alarm. He had hoped to be at the worksite early, but it hadn't worked out. Kyle had woken up just before he was ready to leave and had asked him to look over a quote he was putting together for another job they hoped to score between the sub-trades working here.

Day by day he could see things coming together. It would be a few more months, but if all went well, Carly could fulfill the reservations she had booked.

"That's too bad. How's he doing?"

Derek hesitated. Kyle hated it when Derek talked about his health. Kyle repeatedly told him he wanted nothing to jeopardize their business. He assumed that if the community got wind of how sick he truly was, they wouldn't hire them. Derek never argued with him. He figured many of the people in Millars Crossing already knew that Kyle had cancer. Though not everyone knew how serious it was.

His heart clenched a moment, thinking of what still lay ahead for his brother.

"Not well?" Carly prompted.

He held her gaze, slanting her a melancholy smile as he toyed with her hair. "No. He's not doing well, though he doesn't want anyone to know. A mixture of male pride and hoping people won't always be asking him how he's doing."

"I can see that. It can get a bit tiring. When I had to cancel the wedding—" She bit off the rest of her sentence and Derek tugged lightly on her hair.

"When you had to cancel the wedding," he prompted, "what?"

She paused, as if uncertain how to explain what she was going to say.

"Please, Carly, I don't want you to be so careful around me. We were engaged. We were planning a wedding. It was a big deal. It's no secret that you had a hard time with me going to jail and leaving you behind to take care of everything. Cancel it all. That must have been humiliating and hard. We've talked about this before, so it's not new. I need to know what you were going through. Acknowledge it."

As difficult as it was for him to articulate that, he also knew she needed to know that he understood and took responsibility for the repercussions his actions had had for her.

Her smile showed him how much she appreciated that. "Anyway, when I had to cancel the wedding, it got hard to keep saying the same thing repeatedly, was what I was going to say. So for Kyle, I'm sure he gets tired of it too. I'm sure he doesn't want 'Man with cancer'"—she made little air quotes with one hand—"to be who he is. His only identity."

"You're right," Derek said, once again amazed at how well Carly understood situations. People's emotions.

"And for your information, you also need to know that, though we are kind of sneaking around here"—she looked past him as if to emphasize her point—"I don't want that to be the way it is. I know you and I aren't having a casual relationship to see where things are going. If we're going to do this, I want to do it right. I want to be up-front and direct. And I don't want any secrets between us. Okay?"

Her last words slithered into his conscience. He pulled her close so he wouldn't have to look into her eyes. Wouldn't have to see the conviction in them and respond to her rhetorical question.

"I'm glad you want us to be together," was all he could manage, hoping she wouldn't draw the wrong conclusion from his ambiguous response.

"Me too," she muttered against his shirt, easing out a satisfied sigh. "So, if we're going down that road, I want to start with you coming over for dinner tonight. You and Kyle."

Again, he felt that quiver of apprehension, but behind that a burst of joy. "I don't know if Kyle would be up to coming, but I can ask."

"He's your brother," Carly said. "We used to hang out together."

"Well, I'll be there for sure," he said, giving her an extra-tight hug. "And let me know if I can bring anything."

"No. We've got more than enough cooks. Between Adele, Etta, and me, I think we got things covered." She stayed in his arms a moment longer but then Derek heard footsteps approaching. His name being called.

Pete.

He pulled away and caught a faint grin from Carly.

"Just being professional," he whispered at her. But as he turned to see what Pete wanted, he felt a pinch through the backside of his blue jeans. He hoped he wasn't blushing as he walked toward the entrance. He for sure wasn't looking back to catch Carly's self-satisfied smirk.

But of all the things that had happened between them, it was that one cocky little move that gave him the best indication of how easily they were slipping into the old relationship.

Derek stood on the back step of the large log house, wiping his damp palms down the sides of his cleanest blue jeans.

He was glad he didn't have to come through the imposing front entrance. He'd entered the house through that door whenever he came to pick up Carly for a date. At the time, he suspected Carly's father expected him to do that. A not-so-subtle way of letting Derek know where Carly came from and his expectations for his daughter.

But this time Carly told him to come through the side door that led into a closed-in porch with benches and cupboards for coats and boots.

He fought down a sense of foreboding. Should he have come? Were they moving too fast?

But if he and Carly were starting this relationship over again, he might as well dive in. Get all the "firsts" of this new situation over with.

He sent up another prayer for strength and wisdom. Then knocked on the door.

He heard the squeal of children's voices, a thundering of feet, and then the door swung open. A little girl stood in front of him, her copper curls bouncing around a grinning face. She wore a long purple dress and carried a wand that she pointed at him. "Shazam," she said. "You can't come in until you say the magic word."

"Please?" he ventured, grinning at her.

Another replica of the little girl, either Maria or Maya, Derek was never sure which was which, bounded into the entrance.

"You not apposed to say that," she said, frowning at her sister. Then she turned to Derek. "Maya is bossy. You don't have to listen to her."

"I said Shazam to him," Maya protested, still pointing her wand at Derek.

Maria gave him a reassuring smile. She wore a pink shirt with a glittery heart and black leggings. Obviously, she had a different taste in clothing than her sister did. She held her hand out. "You can come in."

Derek had caught only glimpses of Wyatt's children. He suspected that he and his fiancée Adele, who lived in town but was often here in the evening, had laid down the law about coming onto the construction site. Something he'd been really happy about. It was the one thing that scared the living daylights out of him. The thought that maybe one of the kids would get hurt on the site.

"Nope. He can't," Maya insisted.

Then Carly showed up, a towel tossed over her shoulder, her face flushed. "Maya, I think you can release him."

"He's a prince. Come to capture you," Maya announced.

She wasn't too far off the mark, Derek thought, grinning at Carly.

"You've been watching too much television," Carly said, walking over and kneeling down beside her. "Please don't point that wand at him anymore. It's kind of rude."

Maya narrowed her eyes, as if warning Derek to be careful with her aunty, then she lowered the wand. "I release you," she announced.

"Thank you, my lady," he said with a mock bow.

That netted him a giggle from the princess. Then she and

her sister scooted off, leaving Derek and Carly alone in the now-quiet entrance.

"You can come in now," Carly said, grinning.

He stepped inside and wiped the dust off his boots. "So, just for curiosity, what was the magic word?"

"Today?" Carly shrugged. "Not sure. I think something like Asperanza. Who knows how Maya's brain comes up with these things she assumes we're supposed to know." She gave him a cautious smile. "I appreciate you coming. I'm sorry Kyle couldn't make it."

Out of politeness Derek had extended the invitation to Kyle but had told him he wasn't expected to come. Thankfully, Kyle said he preferred to stay home. Derek suspected Alia was coming anyway. He had wanted to address that issue, but Kyle's pale face and wan features made him keep his comments to himself. He shouldn't care that his brother supposedly had a girlfriend, but he did care if his brother hadn't told her the entire truth about his health.

"He's been pretty tired lately," Derek said.

"I'm sorry to hear that." Carly gave him a sympathetic smile, shot a quick glance behind her, then stood on tiptoe and gave him a quick kiss. "Because that's my only chance tonight," she whispered, then pulled back. "Come on in. Supper will be ready in a few minutes."

"Explain the situation to me?" he asked before she could leave. "Between your brother and their spouses?" People were coming and going, and he didn't know who lived on the premises and who lived elsewhere.

"Oh, none of them are married yet, all engaged though. Adele lives in town but comes here in the evening or Wyatt goes with the three kids there. They're getting married in October. That's when it worked out best for them. Katrina has moved a mobile home onto a property that she subdivided off the ranch and lives there. She and Reuben will move there once they're married. And Etta lives in one of the cabins here. Finn lives in my parent's old house with Reuben. When Finn and Etta get married, they're moving onto a house down the road once it's all fixed up. There was a fire there this summer. Etta was renting it. That's why she's living here. And me, I'm in the trailer."

Derek listened intently, trying to keep up. "But everyone eats here?"

"Only when it works out. It's a transient situation. The only constant is Adele keeps the main house here supplied with leftovers from her bakery. It's always baked that day, and it's fresh, so that's handy."

"Right. Okay." He squared his shoulders as if preparing for battle. "Who's here tonight?"

"Wyatt, Adele, Dean, Maya, and Maria. Etta and Finn and you and me."

You and me. He liked the sound of that, tacked onto the pairings of the rest of her family.

"Carly, are you going to spend the entire night on the porch?" a male voice called out.

Carly rolled her eyes. "Mind your own business, Finn," she called back. Then she turned to Derek. "We should get going. The kids must be getting restless and Finn is probably hungry."

Derek nodded, pulled in another steadying breath, and followed Carly into the kitchen.

A wave of warmth washed over him followed by the buzz of conversation. Wyatt stood at the counter, chopping tomatoes. Finn beside him, cutting up cucumbers.

A tall woman with long brown hair pulled back in a loose ponytail stood by the stove, stirring something that was part of the mouth-watering aromas that wafted through the kitchen. Another woman, a bit shorter, her copper-colored hair pulled up in a topknot, was putting plates on a large wooden table in one corner of the spacious kitchen.

The kids ran back and forth, squealing, until Wyatt reprimanded them at the same time the woman by the stove did.

"So that's Adele trying to keep the kids in check," Carly said. "And Wyatt, you know of course."

"Thanks for coming," Adele said, waving the spoon at him. "Make yourself at home."

Wyatt just raised his hand.

"And here's Etta." Carly nodded to the woman walking toward them, hand extended.

"Hello, Derek," she said, her voice soft, low. "Nice to meet you."

He took her hand, noticing the smears of paint on the back of it.

Etta caught the direction of his eyes and lifted her hand, inspecting it. "Shoot. I thought I got it all," she said, then shrugged. "You can dress me up but you can't take me out."

"That's what I keep saying," Finn said, joining her. He dropped his arm over Etta's shoulders. "So, you're here again," he said to Derek.

Derek didn't miss the faint emphasis on the word *again* nor the way he welcomed Derek. As if he was tolerating his presence. But he knew he had to let it slide and not read more into it than was meant.

"Yes, I am," he said. "Good to be back." He held Finn's gaze, determined not to back down.

Finn's hand slid down and he took Etta's then glanced over at her. "Anything else you need me to do for dinner?"

"Not really," she said. "Thanks for your help."

"Always." He brushed a light kiss on her cheek then looked at Carly. "I think we're ready to eat."

"Perfect." She gave Derek an encouraging smile. "Can you come with me to corral the kids? They might listen better to you than me."

"I'm not so sure about that, but I'm willing to try." He tried not to sound overly hearty. Tried to be casual.

Not so easy to pull off when Wyatt and Finn seemed to be watching his every move.

He couldn't blame them. They'd been hesitant enough to accept his and Carly's relationship the first time around. When he had even less hanging over him than he did now.

For the smallest moment he wanted to defend himself, but he knew that couldn't happen yet. He just had to brazen this out and try not to be defensive.

"It's time for dinner," Carly said to the three kids who were wrestling in the middle of the family room just off the kitchen.

A young boy, about six years old as far as Derek could tell, looked up and grinned. "But I'm winning," he said.

Then the princess, Maya, launched herself at the boy, knocking him over.

"So much for that," Derek said with a chuckle.

"She's not playing fair," the boy muttered.

"That's Dean, by the way," Carly said, walking over to the flailing bodies. "Okay, kiddos, break it up. It really is time to eat, and we're all hungry."

"I'm not," Maya announced, sitting up and pushing a nest of curls away from her face. "I don't need to eat."

"Unfortunately, you do," Carly said. "And we're all ready."

Maria and Dean got up and walked to the kitchen, but Maya stayed behind, kneeling on the floor, her hands on her hips in a defiant gesture. "I'm a magical princess. I don't need food."

"You need some," Carly said, but Derek sensed that she was growing a tad impatient with her stubborn niece.

"What do you live on?" Derek asked Maya, drawn to this little spitfire of a girl.

"Magic and pixie dust."

He made a face. "That doesn't sound near as fun to eat as..." He looked back at Carly.

"Fried pickerel, mashed garlic potatoes, green beans, salad, and doughnuts for dessert."

"See?" he said to Maya. "I think I'd sooner eat that than some dry old dust."

"It's pixie dust," she challenged, but he could tell she was tempted.

"Still sounds dry to me."

She pursed her lips, frowning as if considering this. "But do you know what pixie dust tastes like?"

Derek shrugged, grinning. "It's dust. How good can it taste?"

"Like sparkles," Maya returned.

She was fast on her feet, he had to give her that.

"Well, I think pickerel can be pretty magical too. And even better than pixie dust."

Maya folded her arms. "Well, it could."

"Maybe it's a magical pickerel. Maybe it jumped into Wyatt's boat?"

"Daddy doesn't fish. Uncle Reuben caught the fish."

"Then maybe it jumped into Uncle Reuben's boat."

"Maybe." She seemed to consider this, then heaved out what sounded like a long-suffering sigh. "Okay. I guess I can try the fish."

"That's good. I'm looking forward to trying it too." Derek held out his hand and to his surprise Maya took it, pulled herself up to her feet, and followed along behind him.

"Well, well, look who joined us for dinner," Wyatt said, giving his daughter a level look as he sat down at the head of the table.

"I want to try the magical fish," Maya announced, pulling a chair back. She looked over at Derek and pointed to the empty chair beside her. "You sit here."

"Excuse me?" Wyatt said.

"You sit here...please," Maya conceded.

Derek couldn't stop a flash of humor at the little girl's spunk.

She reminded him of Carly when they first started dating. She could hold her own with anyone.

"How can I refuse such a gracious request," he said, grinning at her as he sat down.

"And Aunty Carly has to sit beside you too. On the other side," she commanded. She shot a quick glance at her father. "Please," she added.

Everyone found a place to sit with Derek and Carly following Maya's instructions. Derek didn't mind. He had hoped he would end up beside Carly. It would give him some moral support.

Wyatt waited a moment while everyone settled down, then he looked around the table, smiling. "It's always good to have so many people around the table. I hope we'll continue to get together once Adele and I are married."

"Four more weeks," Dean announced with a grin. "And I get to carry the rings."

"You certainly do," Adele said, reaching out and taking his hand.

"But now we're going to thank the Lord for this food." Wyatt paused again, then lowered his head.

His prayer was simple but sincere, and it was as if it transported Derek back to one of the few times they had invited him to dinner in this house. Carly's father was still alive, and he was the one who prayed for a blessing on the food and the family. At that time Reuben and Wyatt were both married.

It still felt like the family Derek had always yearned for. The family he and Kyle had found later in their life, with the Kennermans.

After that dinner he'd told Carly how fortunate she was to have her father and her brothers and to have grown up in such a secure family. She'd just rolled her eyes, but he could tell, deep down, she agreed with him.

Now Wyatt was finished praying, and it was as if a switch

flipped. The kids called out what they wanted or, in Maya's case, didn't want. Conversations threaded through each other as people passed food and asked about days.

Derek watched and listened, not daring to say too much. Just enjoying the fellowship.

"Things seem to be coming along nicely on the center," Etta said to Derek. "I know Carly is pleased. There was a time when she wondered if it would even come about."

"No thanks to Alex Rotko," Wyatt said, his tone gruff.

"I just wish it could be ready on time for Adele and Wyatt's wedding," Carly said with a sigh as she scooped some potatoes onto her plate then passed the bowl to Derek. As she did, her hand brushed his, and he felt her foot resting on his beneath the table.

Clandestine connections, he thought.

"Our small wedding party would be lost in that building," Adele said.

"That's what the barn is for," Carly said. "But that won't be finished either. Wasted too much time trying to keep Alex on the ball."

The conversation shifted from the event center to the ranch. Work that needed to be completed. Adele's business. How Katrina and Reuben's place was coming along.

The kids interjected periodically. Dean talked about his teacher and grumbled about a kid in his class who was being mean to him.

Wyatt gave him some advice about walking away. The same advice Thomas Kennerman gave Derek when kids were picking on him.

"Do you have other jobs coming up after the center?" Finn asked Derek.

He pulled his attention back to the moment, gathering his thoughts. "Yes. We're hoping to get the renovation on the grocery store. Getting this job gave us some solid experience for the next one."

"Us being you and Kyle?"

"He takes care of the bids and the phone calls. I do the hands-on work."

"How has he been doing?" Etta asked.

"Up and down. Thanks for asking." He gave her a smile. "We're trying to stay positive."

Before anyone could ask him anything more about Kyle, he turned to Maya. "So, what do you think of the magical fish?"

She gave a laconic shrug. "It's good. I thought it would be better."

"Better? It's amazing," Derek said. He glanced at Etta then Adele. "Very tasty."

"You'll have to give Carly credit for the fish. She said it was your favorite."

Carly gave him a shy smile. "I remember you saying how you and Mr. Kennerman used to go fishing and how much you loved pickerel."

That she remembered created another connection. Another tie to the past.

"I do. I was always so excited when we would go pickerel fishing."

"Where did you go?" Finn asked.

"You know better than to ask a fisherman about his favorite fishing hole," Wyatt said, his tone joking.

They laughed, and the conversation slipped along again.

The longer they sat, the easier Derek felt. The more optimistic.

He glanced sidelong at Carly from time to time and sensed from the gentle smile on her face that she felt the same.

Things seemed to be looking up.

CHAPTER TWELVE

"Come, kiddos. Time to brush your teeth." Adele strode into the family room, heading toward the stairs. "Follow me."

Carly knew from the pout on Maya's face what was coming next.

"Don't want to go to bed," Maya wailed, clutching her Uno cards. "I want to win one more time."

"You already won twice," Maria said, getting up from the floor.

The kids had gathered around the low coffee table in the middle of the family room and had roped Derek and Carly into playing Uno with them while Wyatt, Adele, Etta, and Finn cleaned up.

They had closed the sliding doors between the room and the kitchen. Finn said it was so the kids' noise wouldn't disturb them, but Carly suspected her family was conducting a pre-postmortem.

Once Derek was gone, they would probably come after her and finish the job.

She shouldn't care, but the occasional lifted eyebrow from

Wyatt and the pursed lips from Finn told her that while they were willing to be polite, they weren't letting her off easy.

She wasn't looking forward to it.

"I'm tired," Dean said, yawning as he gathered up the cards from the game.

"I want to play again," Maya insisted, pulling the cards out of Dean's hands.

"Don't do that," Dean said, frowning at his sister. "We need to clean up."

"I want to play again," Maya repeated, louder, just in case no one caught it the first time.

Carly shouldn't care how her niece was behaving, but with Derek sitting right there it was a bit embarrassing.

She turned to Derek, who had been amazingly patient with the kids. Playing Uno and Spot It with them, making sure that they won, but not by too much. Occasionally winning himself. "You play with me," Maya announced.

Derek gave her a slow shrug. "Sorry. I don't want to lose again."

"I let you win," Maya said.

"But I thought you wanted to play so you could win one more time," Derek said, sounding puzzled.

Maya stared at him, as if trying to figure out what had just happened. "But I can win."

"Then I don't get to win."

She narrowed her eyes, then tossed the cards on the table. "You tricked me," she said.

"I'm sorry, I was just teasing you," he said.

Maya stood and looked at him as if taking his measure. "You're a smart man. I like you."

"I like you too," Derek said. "And I like Maria and Dean. You're fun kids and I enjoyed playing games with you."

"Too many games," Carly said, staring pointedly at Maya in case she got any ideas.

"Okay. Bedtime." Maya flounced toward the stairs, giving in but with little grace.

"She's such a drama queen," Dean sighed as he again gathered up the scattered cards.

"No. She's a princess," Maria insisted.

"Okay, drama princess."

Derek chuckled and leaned over to help Dean put the cards in the box.

"Thanks for playing with us," Dean said. "Even if you let us win."

"Did I?" Derek teased.

Dean grinned and followed Adele and the twins upstairs.

"They're fun kids," Derek said.

"They are. I love them so much."

It was just the two of them, but Carly knew that wouldn't last long.

"Well, I guess I better be getting home. I want to make sure Kyle's okay." Derek slowly got to his feet.

Carly got up as well. "I'll walk you to your truck."

"I think I'll be okay," Derek teased.

"I'm sure you will be, but I need to go to my trailer anyway." She tried to sound casual, as if she wasn't hoping they would have a chance to share a kiss. Or two or three. Maybe more.

And that way she could avoid her brothers. For tonight, at least.

"Well then, why don't I walk you to your trailer?" he asked. "That seems to make the most sense."

She smiled, her eyes locked on him.

Watching him with the kids had unleashed an old tenderness. Despite his tough attitude and swagger when she first met him, she'd always been impressed with how he treated his brother and Jason.

How he could be with kids when he met them. Patient, fun, understanding.

That hadn't changed.

He walked into the kitchen and stopped by the table. Etta was wiping the counters, laughing at something someone had said. Wyatt, as usual, had joined Adele upstairs to put the kids to bed.

"Thanks so much for the delicious dinner," Derek said. "And thanks for having me." Carly saw him look Finn's way. Finn just nodded.

Carly knew that if Finn had his way, he would be having a "conversation" with her later. She would have to shut him down. It was none of his business what she did.

But it would be nice if he approved.

"You're welcome," Etta said, tossing the cloth in the sink. "I'd say you're welcome anytime, but this isn't my home, and I'm a guest as well."

"That's dumb. You're family," Finn snorted.

"I guess. Easing my way in." She gave Finn a crooked smile, and his gruff demeanor faded.

Carly couldn't help a flicker of envy at their connection. Despite their struggles in their relationship, Finn and Etta always had the support of the family. Katrina, Reuben's fiancée, had been trying to set them up ever since Etta moved to Millars Crossing.

Derek, however, not so much.

She brushed aside those negative thoughts. She and Derek weren't there yet, but she also knew, as they had talked about, neither of them was looking for a casual relationship. If they were going to spend time together it was with an eye to permanency. To commitment.

So she ignored Finn's penetrating look as she took Derek's arm and walked with him to the entrance and then stepped out of view.

The sun had set and the cool of the evening washed over her

as she walked alongside Derek. He was quiet, and when she looked up at him, he was frowning.

"What's up?" she asked. "You look so serious."

He gave her a tight smile, tucking her arm tighter against him, anchoring her hand beneath his. Claiming her.

"Just thinking..."

"About?" she prompted.

"Your family. Finn and Wyatt don't seem too impressed with me being there. I know they were being polite, but it wasn't hard to read the body language. Or the occasional brotherly frown."

Carly fought down a beat of resentment at his observation. She had been frustrated with her brothers as well, but she understood what they were dealing with. "They're just a few steps behind me," she said. "I wasn't too nuts about seeing you at first either. They just, just have to..." She pressed her lips together, wondering how much to tell him.

"Have to what?" he asked, jostling her arm a little as if hoping to loosen the words.

"Have to get to where I did," she said, looking up at him, smiling her encouragement. "They have to know that you've changed. That you're sorry for what you did. That you want to put it behind you and move on." Even as she spoke, however, she couldn't stop the niggling uncertainty that maybe he hadn't as much to apologize for as she had always assumed.

But what else could she think when he was so adamant that they not talk about what happened.

At first she thought it was because of what she had said. That he wanted to move on.

But lately she'd been thinking he was trying to protect someone.

Kyle? Jason?

She knew she wouldn't be able to talk to Kyle, but Jason worked right on the ranch. She might get to him.

"You look like you're scheming something," Derek said.

"No. Don't be silly, what could I be scheming?" Her words tumbled over themselves, spilling too quickly out of her mouth. Compensating for the guilt she felt.

"How to get your brothers to like me?"

She latched on to his words like a drowning woman. "Well, I might be. But I'm not sure how to go about it."

As soon as she spoke the words, she realized how it sounded. Like she was agreeing with his assumption that her brothers didn't like him.

"I mean, I'm sure they do, in their own way."

"I'm a convicted drug dealer," Derek said, his bald words making her flinch. "I broke your heart and made you cancel our wedding. What else would they think of me being with their sister?"

Carly felt a sudden confusion that shifted too many things for her. She almost refuted what he said, but unfortunately, that much was true. "They'll come around."

She wished she could speak the words with more conviction. "Wyatt wasn't so crazy about Katrina coming back to town when she did. She and Reuben used to date before Reuben married Denise."

"Little different situation. Reuben was a grieving widower and Katrina an innocent business owner."

He didn't know the intricacies of Katrina and Reuben's relationship, and she wasn't about to enlighten him now.

Now, all she wanted to do was focus on how they were going to move forward. She knew her brothers were uncomfortable with her being with Derek, and she knew they would let her know at the first opportunity.

"At any rate, we should give everyone a second chance," she said, as much for his benefit as hers. *Practice for when she talked to her brothers*, she told herself.

"I'm glad you gave me one," he said, turning to smile at her, his eyes glinting in the dusky light of early evening.

They were at her trailer now. She turned to him, slipping into the warmth of his arms. It came so naturally now. So easily.

And despite her previous misgivings about her brothers and their own uncertainties, she lifted her face to his. Moved into his kiss, wrapped her arms around his neck as their kiss lengthened, deepened. Her heart soared and beat in time to his.

She couldn't deny what was happening between them.

And how right it felt.

But even as he pulled away, regret twisting his features, even as she felt a sense of loss at his moving away, she couldn't stop the uncertainty that slid into her heart.

The feeling that she had to sort this all out despite him asking her to leave it alone.

And she knew how she was going to do it.

"Did that flooring company get ahold of you?"

Carly nodded. She pulled her phone out and scrolled through the messages.

She and Derek were perched in their usual spots, each on a sawhorse, across from each other. "They said they would come in a couple of weeks if that worked out."

Derek nodded, frowning, thinking. "The painters should be done in a week while we work on the cement pad and patio outside and on the siding. We'll need to get the gravel hauled in and the outside shed you wanted built." He was quiet, and Carly knew enough by now to say nothing while he mentally and verbally worked through the schedule. It always amazed her what he could keep in his mind, juggling electricians, plumbers, painters, flooring, plus his own workers. "When can you get the staining done?"

"I'm hoping to have it done by next Thursday."

Another nod, another frown. "I think we can get the crew to help you put the beams in on Friday, and we can finish that up by the following Thursday. We'll be installing the cabinets in the bathrooms and the serving areas..." He paused, then pulled out his phone. "I think we're on track for the kitchen to be put together after the flooring is installed."

"I know we are. I can't tell you how much you've taken off my shoulders. There was a time I thought I would lose all my money and all the work done so far."

Derek slanted her a slow smile. "I'm glad that didn't happen." He picked up his coffee and took a sip, his eyes locked onto hers. "This place will be amazing once it's all done. I'm happy your vision is coming to life."

She returned his smile but stayed where she was. This way she could look at him. Think of how much had changed between them since he walked into her trailer over two weeks ago. She just wished she could do what he wanted her to. Put the past behind her. Last night Finn had sent her a text telling her to be careful.

She was annoyed, but it found a place to rest amongst her own vague concerns she wasn't sure she should allow to fester.

"I'm happy too. And now that you've got an extra body, things seem to be moving quickly."

"Jason surprised me. He's working out to be a decent employee."

"Glad to hear that." She clutched her coffee between her hands, looking down. Yesterday she had hoped to "chat" with Jason. She wanted to catch him when Derek was busy, but it hadn't worked out.

A restlessness to talk to him, find out what he knew, had caught her in a grip she couldn't shake.

Derek wanted her to leave it be, and she had tried. So hard. But hearing the way her brothers talked about Derek, seeing the disapproval in their eyes when she talked about him, bothered her. She knew Derek wasn't budging, so she had to try something or someone else. She wanted to clear his name, convinced something else was behind the charges.

Something she could bring to her uncle Gene now that he was back in Millars Crossing.

The sound of a truck pulling up made Derek glance at his watch. "Sounds like the crew is arriving." He got up, took a final swig of his coffee, then walked over to Carly. He bent over and gave her a gentle kiss. So easy. So natural. Just like when they were engaged.

Her heart twisted at the memory, at what they had lost, which made her even more determined to figure out what was going on and why Derek wouldn't tell her who he was protecting. She guessed it was Kyle, but she needed to know for sure.

"I won't see much of you today, though," he said with a tinge of regret in his voice. "I have to take Kyle into town to see the doctor."

"Everything okay?"

"Just a routine check-up," Derek said.

"Okay. Tell him I said hey."

"Will do." He kissed her again, ran a finger down her cheek, then walked away.

Carly bit the corner of her lip as she watched him leave. She would have to make sure she paid attention to when he left. That would be her chance to talk to Jason.

She got back to work, fighting the feeling that she was betraying a trust. Derek had asked her to leave things alone.

But she couldn't.

Just before lunch Derek stopped by, waved at her, then left.

She fought down a flicker of nerves as she walked to the door to watch him drive away. She waited to make sure he was gone, then went looking for Jason. The crew had quit for lunch, but Jason wasn't with them.

Pete told her he was outside, having a smoke.

Even better.

She stepped out of the building and saw him leaning against the large bin Derek had rented to dump garbage and scraps in, sucking on a cigarette.

Carly meandered over, trying to look casual.

"Hey, how's it going?" she asked. Her hands felt clammy with nerves and her heart was racing.

"Going okay," he said, his eyes shifting to her then away.

He took another quick puff of his cigarette then dropped it to the ground and ground it out. "Sorry. Bad habit. He bent over and picked up the butt, holding it between his thumb and forefinger. "I should quit, I know."

"As long as you smoke outside far enough away from everyone else, I won't stop you."

She wasn't sure how to proceed. All morning she had rehearsed what she wanted to say. But now that she was face-to-face with Jason, she wasn't sure how to start.

She shot a quick glance back, but everyone else was still inside.

"I...should probably go back to work," he said.

"That's okay. Stick around a minute. I need to talk to you."

Jason ran one hand down his pants in a nervous gesture. "Sure. But I don't know if I can tell you much. Derek's the one who knows everything. He's kind of the boss, you know. I mean..."

He was nervous. Which made Carly feel like she had a bit of an advantage. She might find out more.

"I know you and Kyle have been friends for a long time."

"Sort of. We got to be friends when they moved in with the Kennermans. I'd been there for a couple of months already."

"They're good people," Carly said, trying to ease his nervousness.

"Yeah. Kyle said he didn't trust them at first. I guess the last

125

place he and Derek were at, they beat Kyle up pretty bad. That's how he and Derek ended up at the Kennermans.'"

"What are you talking about?" This was news to Carly. Derek had always been close-mouthed about his life before coming to Millars Crossing.

"Yeah, it took Kyle a few months before he realized Thomas and Louise were okay and for Derek to relax and not watch them all the time." He released a nervous laugh, as if relieved that this was what she wanted to talk about.

"So has Kyle told you much about some of the other places they lived?" Carly asked. Though this wasn't what she hoped to talk about, she was distracted by what he'd just told her.

"Yeah, Kyle said he thought Derek was going to prison because he beat up the other foster father. It was self-defense, really. Derek wasn't charged. The cops knew about the guy and what a jerk he was."

The word *prison* sent a shiver down Carly's spine. The thought of Derek beating someone up created another claw of apprehension. Were there more things she didn't know about her former fiancé? Other skeletons and secrets in his closet? Why had he never told her?

"Derek always stood up for Kyle, you know," Jason said, smiling now. "Any time anyone tried to do anything to him, Derek was right there. I remember one time in school a kid was pushing Kyle around, thinking he was an easy mark. Then Derek came over. All he had to do was stand there, and the guy backed off. Derek has that way about him. He's a nice guy, he's a great guy, he'd do anything for anybody. Do anything for Kyle. And I think...I think that guy knew that and he backed off. Which was good for Kyle, like I said. 'Course, the guy might have known about why Kyle and Derek got moved from the other foster home."

Jason's conversation was moving in nervous circles, and Carly sensed her opening.

"You said Derek would do anything for Kyle?"

Jason nodded eagerly. "Oh yeah. He's stood up for Kyle all their lives. He's always told Kyle that he's all Kyle has. That the only thing they have is each other. And it's true, they moved from place to place. It was always Derek and Kyle, and Derek you know, like I said, would do anything for Kyle."

"Even go to jail?" Carly asked, homing in on the other thing Jason had said.

Jason nodded eagerly. "Oh yeah."

Carly could only stare at him as what he said settled in her brain.

She grabbed on to an alternative possibility. A possibility that suddenly made a lot of sense.

"Now, talk to me about the drugs," she said, needing to find out what she could while Jason was so chatty. "Where did Derek get them?"

"He said he got them from Tim."

"Did he ever say what he wanted them for?"

"To sell, I guess? I don't know. He never said anything to me, and Kyle didn't want to talk about it."

She kept her eyes on him, her hands planted on her hips, as her mind tested everything Jason was telling her.

"Thanks, Jason, you've been helpful."

"Was that all you wanted to talk to me about? About Derek and Kyle?"

"Yeah. Pretty much." Carly gave him a tight smile. "You can go eat your lunch now. Please make sure you throw that cigarette butt in the garbage."

"Of course. Absolutely. Of course."

Jason scurried away, as if relieved to get away from her.

Carly watched him go, sorting through her thoughts.

Why didn't she think of this before?

Just then her phone buzzed. She pulled it from her pocket

and glanced at the text on the screen then released a hard laugh at who was contacting her.

Uncle Gene was finally in town. He'd gotten her text and wanted to know if she could meet him for lunch.

Of course she could. She could finish up in the barn tonight.

Feeling like things were falling into place, she jogged to her trailer, grabbed her purse, then ran to her truck. Ten minutes later she was on the highway, headed to town. Her heartbeat thumping in time to the frost heaves on the road.

But even as she drove, she felt a niggle of disloyalty to Derek. He wanted to move on and leave the past in the past. Part of her wanted to respect that, but another part of her, the part that resented the reactions people gave Derek, wanted to clear his name.

And then what?

She pushed that question aside. One thing at a time, she told herself.

CHAPTER THIRTEEN

"You look tense," Kyle said when they got into the truck after the doctor's appointment. "You worried about what the doctor said?"

"I'm always worried about what the doctor says," Derek admitted.

Kyle looked ahead with a shrug. "It'll be okay. I know it will."

Derek struggled, once again, with his brother's relentless need to ignore what the doctor said each time they saw him. That Kyle was fortunate to have made it this far. That it was just a matter of time. That his prognosis wasn't good.

Kyle refused to face that reality, and Derek could hardly blame him. He was having a hard enough time himself. He found he couldn't afford to think too much of what lay ahead for his brother. It twisted his soul and broke his heart.

And Kyle's refusal to face the reality tore him in two.

"The project for Carly, it's going good, right?" Kyle asked, clearly wanting to change the subject.

He didn't want to talk about Carly's project right now. He wanted his brother to face the truth so he could support him properly and give him the encouragement he needed.

Encourage him to go back to church instead of hanging out with Alia and telling her who knows what.

"Right?" Kyle prompted.

"Yes, it's going great," he said, giving in. "We'll be ready for siding next week. Then back inside to put in the cabinets after they install the flooring."

"You're on target?"

"Pretty much."

"Good. So why're you so stressed? The doctor said things look good with me, so what's left to be uptight about?"

"Despite what he said, there's lots of—"

"Stop," Kyle said, his voice breaking now as he held up his hand. "I told you we don't need to go there. It does nothing. I know what's happening and I just want to enjoy the time I have left without wondering how long it will be."

"Okay. I get it," Derek returned.

"So, tell me what else is on your mind?"

How was he supposed to break this news to his brother?

"Just tell me. It can't be any worse than knowing I'm going to die sometime."

Derek said nothing, and Kyle punched his shoulder. "Tell me," he insisted.

"Okay, you need to know that Carly's getting close," he said, unable to keep it to himself any longer. "She's starting to ask a bunch of questions I don't know how to answer."

"But I thought you had her convinced to leave things alone?" Despite his bravado over what the doctor had told him, it wasn't too hard to hear the panic in his brother's voice.

"I thought so too."

Kyle looked ahead and scratched the back of his hand. A childhood habit that manifested itself when he was stressed.

Derek looked at the road, focusing on the drive back to Millars Crossing. He was exhausted. It had been a long day. And

Derek knew time wasn't on Kyle's side even though he had already beat all the expectations.

But what hung over his head all the way to Calgary and back was Carly's confrontation and declaration that left him twisted in knots. He loved her so much, cared for her so deeply. He had come so close to telling her everything.

But he was so unbelievably exhausted. So incredibly weary. Juggling his feelings for Carly and his loyalty to his brother.

"You can't tell her." Kyle's voice held a note of desperation. "You just can't."

Derek said nothing to that, knowing that this very thing also laid heavy on Kyle's mind.

Kyle scratched some more, and Derek had to stop himself from reaching over and pulling his hand away.

"Besides, I got a phone call today," Kyle said as Derek fought down the incredible weariness that clung to him. "Before you picked me up."

"Really? Who from?"

Another beat of silence as Kyle worked over his hand.

"Gene Sutton," he said finally.

"Carly's uncle?"

"Is there any other Gene Sutton?" Kyle asked sarcastically.

"What did he want?"

Kyle looked down, as if he realized what he was doing. He pressed his hands against his legs. "He just talked to me. Asked me how I was feeling. Asked me what my prognosis was. Don't know why he cared about that. Said he was retired now and wanted to catch up."

"Was he just making conversation?" Derek felt another sliver of unease. Gene wasn't the type to make casual conversation.

"Seemed like it, so I don't know why he called. It's not like we're good friends."

"And that's all he did? Just asked you some questions?"

Kyle nodded. "Yeah. It was kind of weird. He asked how you were doing. Asked about you and Carly. I told him you guys are getting serious again."

"You did?" The question burst out of him. "Why did you say that to him, of all people?"

Kyle held his hands up, leaning back. "Whoa, buddy," he said. "It sounded like he already knew about you guys. It's not some big Millars Crossing secret. You guys were engaged at one time. What's the big deal that people know you're back together again? We're not going back to the past, right? You did the time and it's over, right?"

Despite his love for his brother and his sympathy for him, Derek felt again that clench of frustration. That annoyance with his brother's easy brushing away of the sacrifice that Derek had made.

"You're not gonna tell them any different? Are you?" Kyle pressed.

On the surface, Carly seemed willing to let the past be in the past. But occasionally he caught Carly looking at him with that question in her eyes. As if she didn't believe him.

He looked again at his brother, the dark lines under Kyle's eyes. His once-bald head was covered with a soft fuzz. In a few days he would have another chemo treatment and probably be throwing up again, the weakness debilitating him.

How could he turn his back on his little brother?

But how could he put Carly off?

"I've always taken care of you," Derek said, easing out a careful sigh. "I won't stop now."

Then, just as Carly had, Kyle rubbed his arm. A small moment of connection between guys.

"You're the best brother I could ever have," Kyle said. He smiled, shoved his earbuds in his ears, and pulled out his phone. Off in his own world again.

Derek turned away, fighting down another beat of irritation blended with anger. Yes, Kyle had always been the weak one. The one who had been so easy to pick on. And yes, he loved his brother and ached for what he was dealing with, but he loved Carly as well.

He thought they could just move on, but now? Carly was growing dissatisfied with his requests to leave things alone.

And now her uncle was back in town. The uncle who, Derek sensed, had never believed him.

Derek rubbed his forehead, pressing his index finger against his temple, hoping to ease the tension headache that had been his steady companion for the past week.

Please, Lord, help me through this. I don't know what to do.

Derek dropped Kyle off at the apartment then left, telling him he was going to pick up some burgers at the A & W for dinner. Or maybe something from Janie's cafe.

Kyle didn't state a preference, so Derek decided on Janie's. Town was busy and he had to park his truck a block away from Janie's and across the street. The air held a faint chill as he got out of his truck, a reminder that fall was coming and right behind that winter. He had to follow up on a few jobs Kyle had quoted to see if they got them. He knew one of the people they were putting in a bid to had been angry with him when he ended up in prison.

But he had to plow on past those community perceptions. Had to hope that his company's low quote would say more than his past.

Money had a certain influence as well.

He glanced sidelong as he was about to cross the street, surprised to see Carly's truck parked in front of Janie's cafe. His heart lifted at the sight. Maybe they could have dinner together. He hurried his steps and was halfway across the street when the door of Janie's opened and Carly stepped out.

Derek was about to call out to her when he saw who followed her out of the restaurant.

Her uncle Gene. He looked serious, and Carly gave him a hug. He patted her shoulder, as if reassuring her.

His mouth went dry at the sight.

What was her uncle talking to Carly about?

Derek moved to stand behind a pickup. Carly and her uncle stood in front of the cafe, clearly having an animated discussion. Then Gene put his hand on Carly's shoulder again, and she shook her head. Derek knew he had to get out of there before they saw him.

He turned and strode down the sidewalk, head down, and ducked into the nearest store, realizing too late it was Wendy's Boutique. And they only sold women's clothing. Too late to duck out now, so he went with it, looking around as if trying to decide.

"Can I help you?"

Derek looked up to see a young woman he didn't recognize smiling at him but looking a bit puzzled.

"Um...just looking around," he said, sidling toward a rack of clothes that announced they were seventy-five percent off.

He flipped through them, hoping he wasn't blushing.

"Those are on sale, so if you see anything you want, just let me know."

She made it sound like he was going to traipse off to the dressing room with a dress over his arm. He gave her a feeble smile, then moved to the window to see what was going on in the street.

Carly was getting in her truck. He couldn't see Gene anywhere.

He waited another moment, mumbled a quick thank you to the puzzled salesclerk, then stepped out the door.

Carly was gone, and while he was relieved he had missed

her, he wished he knew what she had talked to her Uncle Gene about.

How could he bring it up without looking like he was spying on her?

He shook off the thoughts. He would see her tomorrow. Though his crew wasn't working, he had a few odds and ends to clear up. And she was trying to get everything done before his crew came in to put the beams and ceiling boards in place.

He changed his mind about getting something at Janie's and instead went to the A & W. Hopefully his brother would eat something. His appetite had been nonexistent the past week, which was another worry.

He had to put it aside. Trust that the doctors knew what they were doing.

The fact that they had gotten Kyle this far gave him some hope.

Carly brushed the stain over the board, wishing she could stop her brain from spinning.

After talking to her Uncle Gene yesterday, she knew she had to talk to Derek. Had to get the truth from him.

Uncle Gene hadn't fully believed that Derek was the one at fault. Despite giving Derek a warning earlier, he knew Derek had turned his life around. He had told Carly that his money was on Jason but the kid kept insisting he knew nothing so Gene had to go back to Derek being suspect. Carly couldn't imagine why Derek would have gone to prison for someone like Jason. That's when she told Uncle Gene that she suspected Kyle.

Gene had nixed that theory. He had talked to Kyle numerous times, and he didn't budge from his story. Uncle Gene was sure Kyle would have broken if he was involved.

Which left Carly even more confused.

Why would Derek have gone to jail for Jason?

Or maybe Derek had done it after all?

She shook off that last thought. No. That couldn't be. Not Derek. He was covering for someone. She knew it.

The sound of a truck pulling up on the yard broke into her muddled thoughts and sent her heartbeat up a few notches.

Derek. Had to be. She doubted anyone else would work on a Saturday yet.

She pulled in a settling breath, wishing her heart would slow down. Wishing she wasn't so nervous. She was going to confront him and demand to know the truth.

The opening of the front door echoed through the empty building, then his footsteps.

He pushed aside the plastic strips between the barn and the main building and stood in front of her holding his customary two coffees.

"How long have you been here?" he asked with a grin as he walked over to her.

"Couldn't sleep," she said, wrapping the brush in a plastic bag.

He frowned as he set the coffees on a nearby sawhorse, then met her just as she came around the boards.

They met and she slipped into his arms, inhaling the scent of his shampoo, his clean shirt. He always took such good care of himself.

She laid her head against his chest, second thoughts piling onto third thoughts.

Don't go digging. Don't ask questions you don't want the answer to. Why not just leave it alone?

But her uncle Gene's concerns layered over her thoughts. He had been upset when Derek went to jail as much for Derek's sake as hers. He hated the fact that the community had piled on him and rejected him, which made her even more determined to push Derek to tell her what had really happened.

But not just yet. For now, she wanted to enjoy being with him with nothing between them.

Because that was about to change.

"Thanks for the coffee," she said, pulling away from him.

He smiled down at her, tucking her hair behind her ear, fingering it lightly.

"I guess we should drink it before it gets cold." He stroked her cheek with his forefinger.

"I think so." She pulled his head down and stood on tiptoe to give him a soft kiss, letting her lips linger over his, slowly moving over their warmth. She finally pulled back, then, with a slow sigh, she picked up her coffee and sat.

He pulled up another sawhorse and sat down across from her.

"So, how was your day yesterday?" she asked. "What did the doctor say?"

Derek's smile eased off, and he looked troubled. For a moment she wished she hadn't brought up his brother, but it was part of his life and his reality. She wanted him to know that she understood. Was sympathetic. Especially given what she wanted to talk to him about.

"The doctor was pleased with how things were going, which puzzles me, because every time Kyle gets chemo he gets desperately ill. I'm surprised he wants to keep going."

"Where there's life there's hope, I guess," Carly said. She immediately felt foolish. "I'm sorry. The last thing you need right now is clichés."

"That's one thing I'm finding out in this journey. Clichés came about for a reason. There's usually some truth buried in them."

Carly took a sip of her coffee.

"And something tells me you've got something on your mind," he said.

"I do," she confessed. She looked down at the travel mug, twisting her hands around it, wondering where to start. "I met Uncle Gene in town yesterday. He's back, and that's kind of nice." She twisted her hands some more. "We caught up, and he asked me about you."

"And what did you say?" Derek asked.

Carly glanced at him, surprised at the intensity of his question. "I told him we were, well, together, for lack of a better word."

"And, what did he have to say about that?"

"Why are you so defensive?" Carly asked.

"I'm not. I'm just...well, I know I'm not a favorite with your brothers and I know your uncle has been like a father to you since your dad died. I'm just thinking he wouldn't be too crazy about you being with someone he arrested and put in prison. An ex-con who was once a drug dealer."

Carly chewed at her lip. "I don't think you're a drug dealer. And I wish you would tell me what happened that day."

Derek set his coffee down, jumped off the sawhorse and strode away, then back, repeatedly plunging his hand through his hair.

"Don't do this," he said as he paced. "We've been over it again and again. Why can't you just leave it alone?" His hands clenched into fists at his sides as his eyes narrowed.

His anger was like a wave washing over her. Part of her told her to let it go, but her love for him combined with a need to discover the truth outweighed her concerns.

"I can't," she cried out. "I can't sit and watch the way people judge you when I know in my heart that's not who you are." Over and over she heard the condemning words of the man in church. Over and over she caught the sidelong looks from people when they saw Derek. It wasn't hard to guess what was on their mind.

"I got caught, I confessed, and I went to prison. End of story. If you can't deal with who I am, then let me know right now before we go any further."

His voice broke as he spoke, and she saw the pain in his eyes. For a fleeting moment she was tempted to back down. But at the same time, she loved him too much to let this all go away. The way he hoped it would.

Because it never would. She knew eventually her brothers would accept him because she loved him, but she also knew that they would be working with false information. Derek would forever have this cloud hanging over him and she wanted it gone for his sake. The community might forget over time, but she didn't want that stain on his reputation before those things happened.

"I've been chatting with Jason."

"Jason talks too much," he said.

"Jason didn't tell me what happened, but I drew my own conclusions. And I don't think I'm too wrong. Uncle Gene thinks so too. The drugs weren't yours, were they?"

Derek closed his eyes, as if fighting down his impatience with her. He shoved his hands through his hair again then clutched the back of his neck. "It doesn't matter anymore. It's over and done. I just want to move on."

Carly took a step closer to him, rested her hand on his chest, and looked up at him. "I do too, but I also want the truth. I think I deserve at least that much."

Derek's eyes bored deep into hers and fear flickered through her. His hands rested on her shoulders and she felt the tension radiating through him.

"It's not worth it," he ground out. "There's too much at stake."

"What's at stake? Who are you protecting? I'm pretty sure it's not Jason..." She swallowed, wondering if she dared speak the next words. But she was tired of the prevarication, the dancing around the facts.

"It's Kyle, isn't it? It's Kyle you're protecting?" It was the only logical conclusion.

He pressed his lips together as if holding back the words that might've spilled out of him. He shook his head, but she caught a glimpse of fear in his eyes.

She slipped her hands up and wrapped them behind his neck, capturing him. Keeping him from moving away from her. "Uncle Gene never truly believed you were the one who bought those drugs. He told me he tried and tried to get you to change your confession, but you wouldn't. Wouldn't implicate anyone else."

As she spoke she felt a tiny flicker of futility. Would she be able to get Derek to admit the truth?

"It's not Jason, and I can't see you taking the fall for their loser friend, Tim, so that only leaves Kyle." She pushed on, feeling heartless but needing to know the truth.

"Please don't do this," he begged. He tried to pull away, but she locked her fingers, holding him in place.

"You chose to protect Kyle. You chose to go to jail for him, didn't you?"

He said nothing, and now she wanted to turn her hands into fists, beat them against his chest like she had before. Pound the truth out of him. Her frustration simmered into a slow anger.

"Jason said you got the drugs from Tim. That's all I could get out of him."

Still, he remained quiet.

She couldn't stand it anymore. She had tried to be patient.

"Is it because of Kyle's cancer? I know you always took care of him. Were you taking care of him then?" She unlocked her hands and stepped back, her anger growing and filling her. "My uncle thinks you took the fall for someone and I think you did too. I think you took the fall for Kyle because he was sick and you didn't want him to go to jail." Her voice rose with each sentence, her anger echoing through the barn.

"He would have died in jail." The words burst out of him. He lifted his hand, his fingers curled into a tight fist. "It would've killed him. I knew I could survive, but I knew he couldn't."

Carly's anger floated away, like air out of a deflated balloon at his admission. Her legs trembled, and she reached behind her, finding the sawhorse. Her legs couldn't hold her up anymore. She sank down onto the rough wood.

"So the drugs didn't belong to you after all?"

A beat of silence. Then Derek heaved out a heavy sigh and she knew what this cost him.

"No. The drugs weren't mine. They were Kyle's. When your uncle came on the yard, he knew what he was doing. He knew exactly where they were. He went straight to my truck. Someone had told him, and I'm not sure who. Doesn't matter anymore. I told your uncle the drugs were mine. And Kyle went along with it because he also knew what was at stake."

Carly swallowed down a knot of despair. "Kyle never admitted to anything?"

"No. But I was glad he didn't. We both knew I had to take the fall."

Derek dragged his hands over his face, looking spent.

Carly looked at him, her love blending with anger and disappointment. "You went to jail, and I had to call off our wedding. Because of Kyle."

Derek wouldn't look at her as he nodded.

The despair turned to utter sorrow. "You chose Kyle over me?"

Derek's gaze flew to hers, locking in. "I had too, can't you see that? I had no choice."

If she was a bigger person, if her heart was more generous, if she hadn't always seen Kyle as a selfish opportunist, it might have been easier to accept this.

But she had lived with the shame, the anger, the confusion and abandonment of Derek going to prison. All because Kyle couldn't do the right thing. And all because Derek chose his brother over her.

"I told you to leave this all alone," Derek said. "You can't tell anyone. Especially not your uncle. If he finds out that he sent the wrong person to jail, I'm scared of what he'll do. I'm scared Kyle will end up there anyway."

"Stop protecting him," Carly yelled out. "Stop covering for him. I know he's your brother and I know he's sick, but I was your fiancée. I was the woman you were going to commit the rest of your life too. Forsaking all others." She released a harsh laugh. "I know Kyle is important to you, but I thought I was too. You could have at least told me."

"You were important to me—are important to me," Derek corrected. He moved closer, but she held up her hand.

"Please stay away. I've got to work this through. I know I'm sounding selfish and inconsiderate, but why didn't you talk to me about this? My future was on the line too. Why didn't you tell me why you were doing what you did?"

"I didn't dare," Derek admitted. "I knew you were close to your uncle. I was afraid you might let something slip."

"You didn't trust me," she said.

"I was afraid you would talk me out of it."

"I would have," she cried out. "I would have fought tooth and nail for you to stay out of jail."

Derek said nothing for a moment. The silence seemed to expand and fill the space.

"Which meant Kyle would have gone. And like I said, he probably would have died there." He spoke quietly, and by doing so his words held extra weight. "I couldn't let that happen to him."

Carly didn't know what to say. Didn't know what to think. She couldn't say anything to him in the face of what was on the line.

But as she sat there, his words laying out the cold reality of the situation, she knew she couldn't be here anymore.

"You should have told me. You should have trusted me."

She fought down a sob, then spun around and strode out of the building.

CHAPTER FOURTEEN

*D*erek watched her leave, wishing he could go after her.

Change what they had just said.

It was a conversation you needed to have long ago.

But how? When? Was it fair to unburden himself and throw it on her? And what would the repercussions be for Kyle?

His head ached, and he wanted to leave as well, but he had figured on getting some work done.

Carly, however, stayed away the entire day. He kept listening for her to come, disappointed every time he heard a noise and thought it was her.

By the time the day was over, his head felt like someone had slugged it with a sledgehammer.

He hadn't bothered to text her. What they had to say to each other couldn't be expressed with words on a screen.

Though he wasn't sure what he could say to her that hadn't been said over and over and over again. Was he wrong? Had he made the wrong choice?

He had to leave the ranch but he couldn't face Kyle right now. When he got in his truck he called Thomas Kennerman and asked if he could come over. Of course the answer was yes.

He pulled into the Kennermans' yard and, as he turned off the truck, let the sense of coming home wash over him.

This was the place that held his best memories. As he got out of the truck, he felt some of them slip over him.

He and Kyle and Jason playing in the barn, jumping from hay bale to hay bale, laughing and chasing each other, Buster, the Kennermans' malamute, right on their heels.

Camping on the yard in a tent and having Louise bring them hot chocolate and cookies before they went to sleep.

Such an easier and simpler time, he thought, his mind ticking over the events of the past few years.

Now Kyle was sick, the dog, Buster, had passed away, and Thomas and Louise had more gray in their hair. Moved a little slower.

"Hey, Derek, I'm over here." Thomas stepped out of his shop and waved Derek over, one hand holding a welding helmet.

Derek glanced at the house but didn't see Louise's car. She must be visiting her friend, Donna Carleton. The two of them were close and spent a lot of time at each other's place. Derek remembered hanging out with Logan and his little brother Billy when they came over.

Derek walked over to the shop and followed Thomas inside, inhaling the familiar scent of diesel, sawdust, and welding.

"Just finished working on my baby," Thomas said, setting his welding helmet aside.

He patted the tractor parked in the shop, smiling as he did so.

Derek settled onto an old tractor seat set on a metal bar, attached to a frame to stabilize it. He used to sit on it and rock until it bent so far down it almost catapulted him across the garage.

"It's looking good," Derek said in admiration.

Thomas had bought the tractor as an indulgence a few years ago. It was the same tractor he had used as a young boy working on this very place. The same kind his father had used to plow and harvest the crops they grew.

"Runs even better now," Thomas said. He pulled an old wooden chair across the floor with a screech and settled onto it. He reached over to the small refrigerator beside him and pulled it open. "Want anything?"

"I'll have a Dr Pepper if you have one."

"Always," Thomas said, pulling one out and tossing it to him. He took out a can of ginger ale, popped it open and slurped the fizz that bubbled out.

"So, what brings you back to the homeplace?" Thomas asked, tilting his chair back on two feet and pushing his grease-stained hat farther back on his head.

Derek took a sip of the sugary drink and then cradled it, letting the chill cool his heated hands.

"I'm struggling," he said, deciding to come right out with it.

"With Kyle?"

Another sip, another beat of silence to figure out how to speak his mind.

"That and...other things. I've got a lot on my mind right now. What to say to who and how."

That couldn't be any vaguer, but Thomas just sipped and waited.

"Kyle's not doing well," Derek finally said. "It's hard to watch knowing that it's just going to get worse."

"That's always hard news. But I think he's more optimistic than you are. He keeps saying he's going to beat this. When he was first diagnosed, I thought he might. But now..." He was quiet a moment. "What did the doctor say last appointment? Kyle told me you both went."

Derek's head hurt but he had to carry on. "He's dying." The

words were like a jab to the heart. Speaking them out loud to his foster father made them more real.

Derek had always hoped Kyle would beat this cancer.

Thomas nodded, reaching up to swipe at a tear Derek saw tracking down his lined features. His heart ached for Kyle, for himself, and for his foster parents.

"I'm sorry," Derek said. "I should have broken it to you more gently."

"Wouldn't have mattered how you told me," Thomas replied. "I guessed as much, even though Kyle would never admit it."

"I know. I don't know whether to keep reminding him of what's ahead or just let him live in his dream world."

Thomas bent over to pick up a cat that was brushing up against his leg and set it in his lap. He absently stroked its fur as he balanced his chair.

"I can understand that."

"He's failing fast. I lower my expectations of him every day."

"But you still give him work to do, right?"

"Within reason. He does a lot of the bookwork and quotes, though even that's been getting harder, so I don't push him. And as much as he wants to deny what's coming, he's been spending more and more time with Alia."

"Is that a good idea?"

"I don't think she knows exactly how serious his cancer is. I'm fairly sure Kyle hasn't told her. Dream world, remember."

"I understand that. She probably gives him hope." Thomas took another swig of ginger ale. "But it's not fair to her."

"I'm thinking she's watched *The Fault in Our Stars* too many times."

"Didn't watch the movie but I know it doesn't end happy, does it?"

"Nope. I feel like I should tell her the truth."

"No. Not your job. Kyle needs to step up with her and in other parts of his life."

"What do you mean?"

Thomas didn't answer the question right away. He just sat quietly, as if weighing Derek's question.

"Louise and I prayed for you every day you were in prison," he said finally. "Prayed you would be safe. Prayed that you would feel God's presence."

"I did, you know," Derek replied.

"I guessed that from the letters you wrote. Read between the lines." Thomas took another sip of his pop, stroked the cat some more. "We had to do that a lot with you the past few years. Ever since Gene charged you and hauled you off to jail."

Another long beat of silence while the cat stretched and purred. Derek wasn't sure what his foster father expected of him, so he kept quiet, waiting.

"This one was the runt of the litter," Thomas said, obviously meandering off into another topic.

But Derek wasn't fooled. Thomas's thought processes were always firmly anchored. He'd eventually make his way back to what he wanted to say. Derek just had to be patient.

"Got picked on a lot," Thomas continued. "Louise brought it into the house to take care of it. Trouble was, it got so attached to us, it still had a hard time fending for itself when it was time to bring it back here. Even now we have to make sure to feed it separately or it'll starve. But we do it. We are responsible for God's creatures. They depend on us to take care of them. Can be the same with people. But with people, eventually we hope they become independent as they get older." Thomas looked over at Derek. "You always took such good care of Kyle. Always. Maybe too much."

"What are you saying?"

Thomas rubbed his forefinger over the cat's head, but his eyes still held Derek's, as if trying to delve into his soul. "I know you love Kyle, but sometimes love can be taken for granted and can be used as a crutch."

"Kyle has always appreciated everything I've done for him."

"Has he?"

Those two words, that small challenge from anyone else, would have gotten Derek's back up.

"You don't think he does?" he asked.

Still holding his gaze, Thomas' smiled. "You're a giving person. And Kyle is a taking person. I think he's taken too much. And I don't think he realizes how much."

Shock slivered through Derek and he had to stop himself from throwing out the questions now whirling through him.

What did his foster father know? How much? Did he suspect the truth?

He pushed down the worry, slowed his breathing, focused instead on the cat nestled against Thomas.

"Maybe so, but I don't think he's going to change now. All he can focus on is getting through one hour at a time without too much pain."

"I know he's in a tough spot now, but if those are your expectations of him, then that's as far as he'll reach."

Derek wasn't sure he wanted to take this conversation wherever Thomas was going.

He wasn't sure what to say, but the reality was that Carly had already broken through the thin façade he'd been holding up. She'd been angry with him for holding back. And now she had the truth. Could he keep it from Thomas?

He felt as if he were on a runaway train that was gathering speed, headed toward a destination he couldn't change.

Would Carly keep quiet?

Was it fair to keep everything from Thomas?

"I have a feeling you have something else on your mind," Thomas said.

Derek set his empty can on the ground beside him then crossed his arms, rocking slowly on the tractor seat. He pulled in a deep breath, feeling an unexpected shaft of sorrow.

"Not really," he said, still trying to maintain control. Still trying to keep things quiet.

"Secrets and lies can eat you up." Thomas wasn't looking at Derek as he spoke, his focus on the cat. "I know you take things more seriously than Kyle does. It's time he faced his mortality and respected all you've done for him. It will make it easier for him to leave this world in peace."

Derek's heart jumped in his chest and he wondered what his foster father knew.

Carly already knows. You need to tell him.

But he couldn't. Not yet. That would set things off in a direction he knew he couldn't control.

"I think he will," was all he could say.

Thomas just smiled that loving, fatherly smile. Then he set the cat down and, to Derek's surprise, he stood, moved over to him, and gave him a quick hug. Then he held onto Derek's shoulders, looking deep into his eyes. Into his soul. "You are a good person. A godly man. I'm proud of you. I hope you can let Kyle be proud of himself too."

And leaving him with those enigmatic words, Thomas walked toward the door. He opened it and looked back. "You coming into the house? Louise made lemon meringue pie."

Derek sensed the heart-to-heart was over, so he nodded. "My favorite."

"That's why she made it." Then he left.

Derek waited a moment, pondering his foster father's words. Wondering how much he really knew.

Wondering what he was supposed to do with them. What to do with the secrets he'd guarded so closely? So carefully?

Secrets Kyle held as well.

Carly sat on the floor of the barn, weary, worn, and heartsick.

It was dark outside. The building was quiet. The crew had left at five-thirty and, once they were gone, she came here. Saturday, after her confrontation with Derek, she had stayed away. That night she couldn't sleep, so she came to the barn. She stayed until three in the morning, then stumbled back to her trailer. She slept fitfully, dreaming of Derek and Kyle and Uncle Gene.

Tangled, messy dreams that left her feeling worn and ragged when she finally woke up.

By the time she dragged herself out of bed, it was noon. Too late for church, so she worked on the computer. Read a book. Went for a walk.

Avoided her family.

Thankfully, she'd slept better last night. But this morning she had no desire to see Derek, Jason, or the crew, so she waited until they were gone and then went to the barn. She'd been staining for the past four hours and was finished with the last of the beams and boards.

They would need to dry one more day and then they could go up. She had so looked forward to doing that job with Derek and the crew. With watching the set-piece of her center hit the next stage.

Instead, she scribbled out a note and pinned it to the end of the last beam. She could have texted Derek or Kyle, but she didn't know what to say to Derek and couldn't even say anything to Kyle.

She was angry with him. Frustrated with him. Furious that he had let his brother go to jail for him, taking away three years of Derek's life.

Destroying her and Derek's relationship.

Then she felt guilty because she was allowing herself to feel all that anger towards a young man dying of cancer.

Her mind was a swirl of thoughts and emotions she couldn't sort through.

She had shed tears, railed against the unfairness of it all, cried out to God.

She was exhausted and felt she had nowhere to go.

The creak of the door to the center sent her heart into overdrive. It was late and the sun was down. Who could be here? Derek?

Then she heard a female voice, and she relaxed again.

"I'm here, Etta," she called out. "In the barn."

The plastic strips were pushed aside and her friend came in. "Hey there," she said, her voice quiet, as if she was afraid to intrude. "Haven't seen you for a while."

"Have a seat," she said, waving her hand over the dust-strewn floor.

"Don't mind if I do." Etta dropped down beside her, obviously not worried about dust on her paint-splattered jeans.

Thankfully, she said nothing right away. Just sat there in the silence.

"Are you okay?" Etta finally asked. "You weren't in church yesterday."

Carly pulled in a deep breath and laid her head back against the wall of the barn. "No. I'm not okay."

And even worse, she knew she couldn't tell Etta everything that was on her mind.

"Do you want to talk about it?"

"I do. But I can't."

"Sounds mysterious."

"Trust me. It's got all the makings of a Greek tragedy. Or an Italian opera. Which would be the same thing. Except I can't carry a tune."

"Tell me what you can."

She would love to unburden herself to her friend.

"Is it Derek?" Etta asked.

"And what made you jump to that conclusion?" Carly asked.

"Because I came here this afternoon looking for you and he

was short-tempered. Told me he didn't know where you were. On my way out Jason told me Derek had been grumpy all day. And I haven't seen you working here, so I just jumped to the first conclusion that came to me."

"And that was..."

"That you two had a fight."

"Very perceptive of you."

Etta shrugged. "I'm gifted that way." She folded her hands and rested them on her knees, inspecting her fingernails. "So...what was the fight about?"

"So...I'm not telling you," Carly countered, hoping she sounded casual. Indifferent.

"So...why not?"

"Look, we could keep doing this all day, but it's not happening." There was no way she could unburden herself, knowing what she did. Knowing what had happened. Too much was at stake.

If she told Etta everything, she would feel responsible. And if she didn't, she would have to keep holding on to a secret that wasn't hers to keep.

Which is exactly why Derek didn't tell you.

The words resonated through her mind, the truth of them unavoidable.

And yet...

She shook her head, as if she could settle the questions that haunted her. The thoughts she couldn't stop.

"Can't even give me a hint?"

Etta wasn't letting this rest, Carly knew that much. She figured she could give her a bone.

"He didn't tell me the truth. He didn't..." She was going to say that Derek hadn't trusted her. But how could he with what he had done? With what had really happened. "He didn't choose me first."

"That's not good," Etta said, picking at a blob of paint on her finger. "Who did he choose first?"

"His brother."

Etta was silent a moment.

"And why is that a problem?"

Carly realized how petty that sounded, and yet...

"We were engaged. We made promises to take care of each other. Forsaking all others, though we hadn't gotten to that part. Because, well, he made a choice that ruined our plans. Our future."

Etta was quiet, which Carly was thankful for. She didn't need platitudes or empty words.

Her world had been tossed upside down, and she was still trying to find her footing. Trying to know what to do with the truths she had discovered. The burdens she now carried.

"Kyle and Derek were foster kids, weren't they?" Etta asked.

Carly wasn't sure where she was going but nodded anyway. "Yeah. They lived with the Kennermans. They moved here when Derek was about fourteen. Jason lived with them too, for a while. That's how he got the job here."

"Jason? The kid who probably got the drugs Derek was accused of owning?"

"The drugs Derek admitted to owning," Carly corrected, though she knew that wasn't the entire truth either.

"I can't believe Derek hired him."

"He wanted to give him a chance," Carly said, sighing, wishing she could get rid of the pressure in her brain.

"Big of him," Etta said. She picked another blob of paint off her fingers, frowning. Finally she spoke again. "So, is there any chance for you two? I mean, you seemed to be pretty in sync. And now that I've found Finn, I recognize in sync."

"As in the boy band?" Carly said, trying to divert her friend's painful line of questioning. She and Derek had lost each other once. Now it had happened again, and she didn't know how to face it. Humor was her only defense right now. Or tears, but she had shed enough of them the past few days.

Etta elbowed her in the side. "You know what I mean."

Carly sighed. "I do. Derek and I always had this connection. From the first day we started dating. I thought we'd always be together. And then everything fell apart." She pressed her lips against an unwelcome surge of sorrow. "And now..."

"How long are you going to stay mad at him?" Etta asked. "Do you think you can find a way through all of this...trouble, or whatever it is?"

Carly's heart contracted as she thought of what lay ahead. It had only been two days and already she missed Derek. She had closed her heart off to him for three years, but as soon as she opened it up, she had allowed him to enter fully and completely.

And now, she was back to where she'd been over three years ago.

Angry with him and his betrayal and soul-achingly lonely.

"I don't know."

"Can you reconcile with him?" Etta turned her head, looking directly at Carly.

"I don't know."

"I remember how devastated I was when I thought Finn didn't want me around. When he was so upset that I hadn't told him everything about Allister. It was hard for me to open up to him. To trust him."

"But Derek and I were going to get married," Carly said. "We had a solid relationship."

"Which means you should be able to find a way back to each other again."

"I'm so confused right now," she muttered. "I always knew exactly what I wanted. How I thought I should behave. Now I'm not so sure anymore."

The burden of knowing what had happened weighed like a stone on her shoulders.

She wanted nothing more than to pour her heart out to Etta. To ask her what she should do.

But it wasn't her secret to share.

It was Kyle's.

Carly pulled in a deep breath as her hazy thoughts coalesced.

Kyle's secret. He was the one holding on to it. He was the one who needed to release it.

"I know what I need to do," she said.

She got up, brushed the sawdust off her pants, and held her hand out to Etta.

"Thanks for coming by."

"Okay, I guess?" Etta said, sounding as puzzled as she looked.

"Really. I appreciate the support. I need to take care of something. In private," she said to Etta.

"Okay, then. I'll leave you to it." Etta gave her a quick smile and walked out of the building.

Carly waited until she was gone, pulled her phone out of her pocket, and glanced at the time.

Too late to call.

And she didn't want to risk Derek answering Kyle's phone.

She needed to go into town for groceries tomorrow.

She could stop by the apartment then while Derek was at work.

Hopefully Kyle would be home.

If not, she would find him. One way or another, she was going to have a little chat with him.

CHAPTER FIFTEEN

"Thanks for supper," Derek said, setting his knife and fork on his plate then wiping his mouth with his napkin. "That was good."

Good was a bit of an exaggeration, but the fact that Kyle had even made supper was quite a feat. "It's nice to come home to something to eat."

"I'm feeling better, so I was hungry too."

"Haven't seen much of you the past few days."

Saturday, after his visit with Thomas and Louise, Derek had returned to the apartment, determined to talk to his brother.

But Kyle was gone. He had left a note telling Derek that he was with Alia at a movie.

Kyle had left his phone behind, so Derek couldn't text him.

Sunday the same.

Monday Derek took him for chemo. There was no way he was confronting Kyle after that.

Derek had heard Kyle throwing up last night. He knew he couldn't talk to him this morning, knowing how rough his brother's night had been.

It was now Tuesday evening. He hadn't seen Carly since

their face-off on Saturday. She had missed church and had stayed away during the day. He knew she was working, because yesterday and this morning he'd seen that she'd stained more of the beams.

"I've been doing my own thing," Kyle said with a shrug.

Derek wondered what he meant by that but decided not to follow through. He had other things on his mind and he didn't want to end up diving down some rabbit hole of Kyle's making.

"So, you were with Alia this weekend," Derek said, glancing over at Kyle's still-full plate. The entire meal he had just picked at his food, taking a few bites. He was looking extra pale now, and for a moment Derek wondered if he should keep on with the conversation he wanted to have.

"Yeah. She's a great girl."

"She seems nice."

Kyle gave him a sharp look. "You sound like you're patronizing me and her. She is really nice."

"Not patronizing at all." Derek leaned back in his chair, resisting the urge to cross his arms. *Defensive gesture*, he reminded himself. "I think she's a good person."

"She is. I like her." Kyle got up to clear the table, ambling to the kitchen with some plates.

Derek stayed where he was, watching his brother's tentative motions. He was getting weaker. Just as the doctor had said would happen.

He felt bone-weary from carrying all the worries and emotions of not only the past few days, but the past few years.

In prison he'd worried whether Kyle would be alive when he got out. He worried about keeping himself out of trouble. Constantly watching his back. He worried about Carly. Worried about what she thought of him. Worried about what her family thought of him. He worried about his foster parents, hoped they were doing okay.

He had carried so much for so long. It was too much.

For a few weeks he thought his life had found a level spot. A place of peace.

Even though, threaded through all of that, was the fear that someone would find out the truth.

And now that Carly's uncle was back, now that Carly had figured out for herself what happened, he had even more to be concerned about.

Trust in the Lord and lean not on your own understanding. In all your ways acknowledge him and he will direct your paths.

The Bible quote was truth distilled, he knew, but trusting was easier said than done.

God's word had sustained him in prison. Prayer and connection with the Lord had pulled him through the lonely desolation of those years.

He thought he had "fixed" everything when all he had done was postpone the inevitable.

At least Kyle hadn't gone to jail.

But he still might.

Later, he told himself, pushing that thought down. *Deal with that later.*

"Have you told Alia everything about what you're facing?" Derek asked.

Kyle came back to the table and picked up the half-full pot of stew. He avoided Derek's gaze and shuffled back to the kitchen.

Derek let him putz around in the kitchen, giving him time to think about the question.

When he finally came back to the table, Derek pushed again. "Have you told her the truth about your prognosis?"

Kyle dropped into a chair across from Derek, his head down, staring at the table. He shook his head. "No. She knows I'm sick."

"Does she know you're dying?" The harsh words seemed to echo in the room, their stark reality coming to rest in the silence.

"I'm not dying. I'm not!"

Derek choked down a twist of frustration at his brother's outburst. Something Thomas said came back to him.

He needs to step up. In more ways than one.

"Are you ever going to tell her?"

"I'll beat this," Kyle said. "I'll get through this. I really like her."

"If you care for her, then you'll tell her what you're facing," Derek said, choosing not to indulge Kyle's optimism. Not anymore.

Kyle looked down at the tablecloth, pleating and unpleating it with trembling fingers. "I can't. She'll break up with me. And I...I've already lost so much. Given up so much."

Despite his sorrow for his brother's situation, Derek stifled a burst of anger.

Tell me about it, he wanted to say.

He'd lost his fiancée, three years of his life. He lost the hard-earned respect of Carly's family, of his community. He'd lost his livelihood and was only now working his way back. And Kyle dared to talk about what he'd lost.

He's dying.

The truth Derek could never get past.

He had hoped to keep the truth about the drugs from Carly. Deep down he'd hoped that he could eventually tell her.

After Kyle was gone and the threat to his brother's freedom was erased.

But it was slipping out now.

The truth will set you free.

Derek rubbed his hand over his face, blinking, his eyes like sandpaper from lack of sleep. From carrying the worries and concerns.

From grieving, once again, the loss of Carly.

"I know it's hard to face, but it's not fair to her to keep

160

stringing her along," he finally said, his voice gentle but firm. "In at least one part of your life, be truthful."

Kyle looked up at him, his eyes narrowed with anger. "You can't ask that of me," he said. "It's just not fair."

Derek was suddenly tired of trying to make his brother see reason. Tired of endlessly trying to push this rock uphill.

"It's not about fair. It's about what's right," he snapped.

He was about to say more when his phone rang and his heart jumped. He pulled it out of his pocket. It wasn't Carly.

Just Pete.

Kyle got up. Derek wanted to stop him, but while he spoke to Pete about the project, his brother left the apartment.

Derek wanted to follow him to see where he was going, but when he looked out the window, he saw Kyle driving away.

Carly yawned as she pushed her cart down the grocery aisle. She was so tired it was hard to concentrate. All day her mind had flip-flopped between her conversations with Derek and her conversation with Etta.

She knew the truth now, and it alternately made her furious and heartsore. She'd been carrying the burden of the information since Saturday. And she felt as if she was no further ahead in what she needed to do. She just knew she still loved Derek. Deeply, despite the choices he had made.

What would you have done?

What if it was Finn?

But she couldn't imagine her brother sick and wasting away. Couldn't imagine herself having to choose between marrying Derek and Finn going to jail. Couldn't imagine Finn letting her take the fall without a fight.

Too much to think about. Her head hurt. Her heart ached.

With another sigh, she glanced down at her list, forcing

herself to focus. Adele had found out she was going to town and asked her to pick up a few things for her.

Okay. Black beans, garbanzo beans, and brown beans. She grabbed a few cans of each off the shelf and deleted them from the list on her phone. Next up, pudding for the kids. Not here, unfortunately. Probably a few aisles over, so before she left this one, did she need anything more? She glanced up and down, looking backward as she pushed her buggy around the corner and narrowly avoided crashing into another cart.

She jerked her cart back, forcing an apologetic smile as she looked up.

Just in time to see Kyle Gilbert staring at her, clutching a paper list.

He looked even more gaunt than he did the last time she saw him. Exhausted and wrung out. Despite her simmering anger with him, her heart contracted with sympathy as he looked up at her, dark circles like bruises below his wide eyes.

"Hey you," she said quietly, as if afraid to startle him more than she already had.

"Hey yourself." He returned her smile, his hands kneading the handle of the cart. "I thought I saw you earlier."

She wasn't sure what to say. He wanted to make small talk. But the kind of talk she really wanted to have with him was anything but small. It was huge. Life-changing.

"I couldn't keep up to you," Kyle said. "You were marching triple-time. Like you always do."

His easy reference to the past pulled up memories of him trying to keep up to her and Derek as they went for a walk. The one time they took him to West Edmonton Mall and he complained that Carly was going too fast.

"Yeah. Always on to the next thing," she returned.

He was quiet a moment, as if unsure what to say. She knew what she wanted to say, but this wasn't the place.

"Derek says the event center is coming along pretty good,"

he said, as if determined to keep her talking to him.

"Yeah. I'm pleased."

"That's good. I've been helping. Well, as much as I can." He gave her a sheepish look. "It's the least I can do. Derek has always been a good brother to me."

Carly pressed her lips together, fighting down the urge to tell him that Derek had been far too good a brother to him. Tell him that he had taken his brother for granted.

"He's a good guy, you know," Kyle said. "What he did...he knows it was a mistake...he knows it was wrong. He more than paid the price for it all."

Carly stared at him, aghast. How could he look at her and blatantly lie like that? How could he talk so piously? Act so self-righteous?

"Are you kidding me?" she finally said.

Kyle blinked, staring at her. "What do you mean?"

"You need to tell me what really happened," Carly said, unable to hold it in any longer. "That day Derek got arrested."

Kyle stared at her. "You can't say anything. You can't..."

What was he talking about?

Then Kyle pressed his hand to his chest, breathing heavily. He looked increasingly pale. In fact, he looked like he was about to faint.

Carly moved closer, and his eyes rolled up in his head.

She didn't think. Just reacted and caught him before he hit the cement floor of the grocery store.

Kneeling on the floor, her heart thundering in her throat, she yanked her phone out of her pocket. Her hands shaking, she tried to dial 911. When the operator came on the line, she forced herself to speak clearly. Forced herself to be calm.

In the meantime, someone else came upon them and dropped to the floor beside her. Tall, broad-shouldered, longish blond hair.

"What happened?"

"He just fainted," Carly said. "He has... He has cancer." She struggled to get the words out over the pounding of her heart.

"That's Kyle Gilbert isn't it?" the man asked.

Carly nodded.

"We gotta get him to the hospital," he said.

"I just called 911 and an ambulance is on the way."

"We can get him there faster than they can," he said. He bent over and took Kyle's pulse then checked his pupils. "I'm Morgan Price. I'm an EMT."

Morgan pulled his keys out of his front pocket and handed them to her. "We'll take my truck," he said.

Before she could register any protest, he picked Kyle up and strode down the aisle, people gaping at them.

Carly grabbed her purse and followed Morgan out of the store, praying as she scurried to keep up.

She needed to let Derek know, but they were at Morgan's truck before she could pull her phone out.

With trembling fingers, she clicked the fob Morgan had handed her.

"Open the back door," Morgan said, his voice brisk.

She did so then hurried around to the driver's door as Morgan laid Kyle on the back seat, got in, and shut the door behind him.

She started the truck and backed it out, forcing herself not to rush.

But Morgan was right. They made it to the hospital in less than a minute. Carly pulled up to the emergency entrance. Morgan had called ahead to the hospital to let them know they were coming and what had happened. She envied his calm assessment. Her hands were slick with sweat, her heart hammering in her throat.

As he stepped out of the truck, two people came running toward them with the gurney. With quick efficient movements, they strapped Kyle onto it and pushed him into the hospital.

Morgan stuck his head in the truck. "Just park this," he said. "I can take you back to your car later."

Carly nodded and, after he closed the door, she drove to the parking lot.

She parked, shut the truck off, pulled in a deep breath, then got out her phone.

Derek answered on the third ring.

"Hey, what's up," he said, his voice brusque. Indifferent.

"Kyle's in the hospital," she blurted out before he could say anything more.

"What? When?"

"Just now. I was with him in the store—"

But she couldn't finish her sentence. Derek had hung up.

She put her phone back in her purse then blew out her breath, trying to calm herself. Derek was coming, and she wasn't sure she wanted to face him.

And yet, his brother was in the hospital. She couldn't leave Kyle unattended.

She got out of the truck, her heart heavy as she trudged toward the hospital. This morning she had woken up full of plans. She was going to get some groceries. Then she was stopping at Derek and Kyle's apartment. She was going to talk to Kyle. Calmly. Clearly.

And now?

She pushed open the door of the hospital and stepped inside, looking around.

She saw Morgan talking to the receptionist. He turned when she came nearer. "They're still trying to stabilize him," he said.

Carly nodded, not sure what to do. Stay? Leave?

"I can take you to pick up your vehicle," Morgan said.

"That's okay. It's not far. I can walk if I have to. I'll stay until I know what's going on."

"Okay. Then I'll hit the road."

"Thanks for your help," she said.

"All part of the job," he returned with a crooked grin. "Even if I'm not on the job."

Just then the door of the hospital opened and Derek entered. He looked around, saw Carly, and strode over to her.

"Where's Kyle?"

"Still in the ER," Carly said, suddenly breathless in Derek's presence.

He closed his eyes, dragging his hand over his face. He looked exhausted. And her heart pleated at the sight.

"Do they know anything?"

"I was on the scene when he collapsed," Morgan put in. "Not sure what caused it."

"He's got brain cancer and has been feeling really weak lately. He's my brother."

"Okay. They're stabilizing him right now. Not sure what they're doing, but the doc will tell you more when she comes out." He turned to the receptionist. "Can you let them know Kyle's brother is here?"

The receptionist nodded then got up and left them.

"I'll go now," Morgan said, then turned to Carly. "Are you sure you don't need a ride back to the grocery store to get your vehicle?"

"I'm okay," she said. "Thanks again for the offer."

"Any time." He gave her a grin that seemed to suggest he wanted to do more than offer her a ride, but she gave him a polite smile and turned away, hoping he got the hint.

He must have, because without another word, he left.

She wasn't sure what to do, but despite the distance that yawned between her and Derek, she didn't want to leave him alone.

"I'll wait with you," she offered.

"That'd be nice."

An awkward silence fell. Carly walked over to the chairs in the waiting area and sat down.

166

Derek sat down in a chair across from her, leaning forward, his clasped hands resting between his knees. He drew in a long, slow breath, then, after another long pause, looked up at her.

"Does it help to say I'm sorry?"

Carly struggled with the myriad of emotions she was dealing with.

"I don't know what that will change."

Derek heaved out a heavy sigh. "I don't know either. Thought it was worth a try."

She had so much she wanted to say. So much that was ready to spill out.

But she wasn't sure how to bridge the gulf between them.

"So, what are you going to do?" he asked.

She stiffened. "Nothing. For now." She was carrying this information, and she knew what the repercussions would be if she were to share it with her uncle.

"I'm sorry you have to deal with this," he said. "I'm sorry you have to make a choice. It isn't easy."

His words burrowed into her soul and took root.

Could she tell her uncle the truth?

Could she keep holding it to herself?

Either option would create a strain with her and Derek if they stayed together.

Either option would keep them apart.

The sorrow created by her thoughts lodged like a cold stone in her chest. She stood, feeling like she was abandoning him but unable to stick around. "I'm sorry," she said, breathless. "I thought I could stay, support you..."

"I get it."

She looked at him once more but then, with a shake of her head, walked away. She felt like a coward, but at the same time, she didn't know what she was going to do moving forward. What to keep quiet about.

What to say.

CHAPTER SIXTEEN

"*How* ow are you feeling now?" Derek hovered over Kyle's bed, forcing a smile as he met his brother's sunken eyes. Yesterday, after they took him out of the ER and admitted him to a room, Derek had been convinced they were at the beginning of the end. Convinced Kyle would be stepping over the threshold of death that had lain ahead of him the past almost four years.

But yet, here he was. Diminished, but still here.

Derek swallowed down a sob and took his brother's hand gently in his.

"I'm okay," Kyle said. He looked past Derek to where Thomas and Louise hovered. "Hey, Dad, Mom."

Louise and Thomas came to each side of his bed, touching him, connecting with him, comforting him.

"Hey, you," Louise said.

They stood around him a moment as Kyle looked from one to the other. "I guess I'm still here." He flashed them a weak smile and, despite the gravity of the situation, Derek had to smile.

"Yes. You are."

"Told you I'd beat this," Kyle said, sounding more confident than he looked.

Derek said nothing. Now was not the time. Besides, what difference did it make?

As he looked at his brother, all the things he wanted to talk to him about seemed pointless. And yet...

"The doctor said I can go home tomorrow," Kyle said. "Told me just to take it easy." He gave Derek a sheepish look. "And I left the groceries at the store. Sorry."

"Don't worry about them," he said.

"We can pick them up when we go home."

"I told you not to worry about them."

There were much bigger things they needed to discuss. All the way here he had rehearsed what he was going to say to his brother. To his foster parents.

He had hidden the truth long enough.

It needed to come out.

But now, standing by his brother's hospital bed, seeing the stark reality of what was ahead for him, Derek choked. He couldn't say what he had come to tell his brother.

Again, he felt that push-pull of love for Kyle and his love for Carly. That tug of war that kept him awake at night, trying to find comfort in his prayers. Some direction.

"Do you need to go back to see the doctor once you're discharged?" Louise asked. Ever the practical mother.

"Yeah. He wants to see me in a week. Run a bunch more blood tests. I can't believe I even have any left after all the prodding and poking they did here."

Derek had hoped to talk to the doctor but was afraid it would be more of the same.

Wait and see. He's doing well, all things considering. It's a matter of time.

All the same platitudes every doctor trotted out whenever they met with them.

169

"Derek tells me you've been seeing a young woman. Alia," Thomas said, pulling up a chair for Louise, then one for himself.

"Yeah. She's great," Kyle said, smiling widely.

"I hope we can meet her sometime," Thomas said.

"Me too." Kyle's smile faded a little though.

"Maybe we can have her over for dinner when you're out." From the serious expression on his foster father's face, Derek guessed that Thomas had a deeper purpose than mere chitchat about Kyle's girlfriend.

Thomas leaned closer, then took Kyle's bruised hand in his, running his thumb over the marks where the nurses had tried, unsuccessfully, to start a couple of IV's.

"Does she know?" Thomas asked, going for direct. Straightforward.

"About what?" Kyle asked, sounding surprised. But Derek could see from the way his eyes darted away from all of them that he knew exactly what Thomas referred to.

"Have you told her your prognosis?"

"I told you, I'm going to beat this," Kyle snapped.

Derek couldn't be quiet any longer. "I'm glad you're so positive about this, Kyle," he said. "But you know and I know what the doctor has said."

"They've been wrong before."

"Yes, you've already beaten the odds." Derek moved closer to his brother, settling on the edge of the bed to get closer to him. "You're a fighter and I'm so thankful you are. I'm so thankful I've been able to work with you the past few months. Not going to lie, I didn't expect that when I left for prison. I prayed for many things while I was there, but my main one was that you'd still be here when I got out. And here you are. And I feel that God has given us the gift of extra time."

Kyle blinked, biting his lip.

"We're thankful for every day we have with you," Thomas

put in. "But I think we all know you're living on borrowed time."

"Don't say that," Kyle said, but the snap had gone out of his voice.

Derek hated this. Hated bursting the bubble his brother had carefully constructed around himself. But right now, there were more things at stake than his brother's feelings.

"You need to tell Alia," Derek said, gently placing his hand on Kyle's arm. "It's not fair to her to let her think you're going to get better."

"What does it hurt to not tell her?" Kyle protested, pulling his arm away. "If she doesn't know—"

"It's not right and it's not the truth," Thomas said. "And it's rather selfish."

Kyle ignored them both, scratching at his hand.

"I know you're hoping to get better and honestly, I've been hoping too," Derek continued. "But you know as well as I do what Doctor Belkin has been telling you." The words sounded harsh, but Derek knew they had to be spoken aloud. They had to be faced. "Like Thomas said, it's selfish to let Alia think she might have a future with you."

"But she'll break up with me."

"Then that's the way it is," Derek said. "You need to face the truth. In more ways than one."

Kyle's expression took on a look of terror. "What are you saying? What do you want me to do?"

Derek glanced over at Thomas and Louise, who were looking at Kyle, their faces wreathed with sympathy. After his conversations with Carly and then Thomas, Derek knew it was a matter of time before the truth would come out. For the sake of his brother, he wanted to hold off as long as possible.

And yet—

"Nothing right now," Louise said. Slowing things down. The

mother in her intervening at the moment. "Right now you need to focus on getting stronger."

Thomas frowned at Louise, and Derek could tell that he didn't think she was helping matters. But Derek was hesitant himself to push too hard.

Things had waited this long. Surely they could wait until Kyle was ready.

Carly knows.

The two words pierced the fragile defense he had put up.

Not only did Carly know, Derek was suddenly weary of the subterfuge. Of protecting Kyle.

But he's dying.

And right now, so was Derek. Dying a little more every day. With every moment he was apart from Carly. With every condemning look he got from locals. With every time he felt he had done too much for a brother who didn't seem to realize or appreciate the sacrifice.

He thought of Carly and how angry she was that he had kept all of this from her.

She deserved to have the truth come out. Though he didn't know if it would make a difference.

"You just rest," Louise said, patting Kyle's arm. "We'll come back again tomorrow." She got up and brushed a kiss over his pale cheek, then nodded at Thomas and Derek.

They took the hint, said their good-byes, and left the room.

"I think we need to go get some coffee or something," Louise said. "We can go to the Inn. We can walk there. Janie's is probably closed at this time of night."

"Too bad," Thomas said. "I was craving one of her pecan bars."

"We can satisfy that craving another time." Louise flashed her husband a smile as she tucked her arm through his. Thomas smiled down at her, and as he watched them Derek felt a quiver of jealousy.

Their relationship was the kind he had hoped to have with Carly. At one time, they'd been on their way to that goal.

Then...then Kyle made yet another dumb choice.

The night air was cool and Derek strode alongside his foster parents, thinking about the work that lay ahead of him yet. Crossing Construction had, to his surprise, been awarded the contract for a house that would keep them busy for the next few months. As well as a few basement reno's which would be perfect for winter.

The business part of his life seemed to be looking up despite his reputation.

As for his love life—

"You're looking pensive," Louise said, her voice laced with sympathy. "I imagine seeing Kyle in the hospital is difficult."

"It is. Though he's always a lot more optimistic about it than I am."

"Always was a dreamer," Thomas said. They walked up to the door of the Inn and Thomas held it open for them to walk through. A few patrons were scattered around the dining room. A couple in one corner and a group of women against the wall, laughing and chattering amongst each other. Derek recognized Dot Westerveld and her sister-in-law Tilly.

Dot waved hello to Louise as they wove through the empty tables to a booth against the wall.

"You don't want to join them?" Derek teased his foster mother as they sat down.

Louise's expression was serious as she shook her head. "No. We have important things to talk about."

Derek's heart fluttered as he looked over at Thomas, who was equally serious.

"So, when were you going to tell us the truth about why you went to prison?" Louise asked.

Derek felt as if the horse he was riding had suddenly bolted and all he could do was hang on.

Carly knocked on the open door of the hospital room, then stepped inside. The nurse at the desk had said that no one was there yet, though Carly had gotten a text from Louise, asking if they could meet in the hospital. In Kyle's room.

The privacy curtain separating the two beds in the room was open and she could see Kyle, sleeping now. No one else was here yet.

The window of the room overlooked a courtyard that held bushes and a few late-flowering lilies.

At least he has a nice view, she thought.

She stilled the questions, stopping at the foot of Kyle's bed. He looked even more pale than when he collapsed in the grocery store, his eyes ringed with dark smudges, like a bruise. His cheeks hollow.

But at least he wasn't hooked up to anything.

He opened his eyes as she looked at him, blinking a moment. Then his expression grew fearful.

"What are you doing here?"

"Came for a visit," she said, keeping her tone light, easy. "How are you doing?" No sooner did she ask that than she felt foolish. Not too hard to see how he was doing.

Not well.

He waved his hand around. "I'm doing super."

Still cocky, she thought, fighting down a beat of annoyance.

"But I'll be out soon. Doc said I can leave tomorrow."

She heard footsteps coming toward the room. She looked back over her shoulder, hoping it was Louise. But the nurse kept walking.

"Things going okay at the event center?" Kyle asked, stifling a yawn. "Derek hasn't been telling me much lately. Just that things are on schedule."

"They're going okay." Today she guessed they would put up

the wood she'd spent so much time staining and finishing. She had wanted to be there, but that meant facing Derek, which was too painful and humiliating. Even seeing him the other day hadn't helped. Had only made her more confused and frustrated, so she'd stayed away.

She would check it out tonight. When everyone was gone.

"Just okay?" Kyle closed his eyes a moment and Carly wondered if she should wait for Louise. But he pulled in a deep breath and opened his eyes again. "Derek's been a real grump lately," he said. His voice held the faintest question. As if he was hoping Carly could enlighten him.

"Probably just tired. Worried about you." His words built a tender yearning. Was he grumpy because of their fight?

She wanted nothing more than to breach the gulf between herself and Derek, but she wasn't sure how. Not as long as he held on to the secrets he did.

Kyle shook his head. "Nah. He's been like that since Saturday, which is weird, because he'd been singing and whistling for about a week before that. I thought maybe the two of you had made up."

And what was she supposed to tell him about that? She let it slide, wishing Louise would show up. She pulled up a chair and sat down, close to Kyle.

"Did you? Make up?" Kyle's voice held a wistful tone that surprised Carly. "I mean, I was really hoping you would."

"Why?" Carly couldn't stop the question. "Why did you hope that?"

"Well, you know, you guys were going to get married. And then, well, he went to prison, which sucked." Kyle lowered his eyes, rubbing his forehead with one hand. "But now, he's out, and he's working, and I know he's always loved you. He never said much in the letters he wrote me, but he wrote Mom and Dad and he told them. So that's not cool. That you guys broke up. He's a great guy, and if you guys get back together, then that's a good happy ending."

Kyle's defense of Derek shouldn't surprise her, but it also stoked the simmering anger she'd felt for the past few years. Anger that had, at one time, been directed to Derek but now had a different target.

Seriously, Carly, how can you be angry with a young man dying of cancer?

Her thoughts condemned her, but at the same time, this was her reality. The man lying on the bed had caused her breakup, sorrow, and humiliation. And he acted as if it was a mere inconvenience.

"He is a great guy. Very self-sacrificing. And you should know." She let the sentence hang between them, hoping he would get the subtext in her voice.

Kyle stared at her, his eyes wide. "What do you mean? What do you know?"

Getting warmer.

Carly wanted to hit him with a resounding "Everything" but that was rather dramatic. She didn't want to make him faint again.

"I know that Derek is hiding something. Can you tell me what it is?" She wanted to tease the truth out of him. She wanted him to be the one to tell her.

"I don't know what you're talking about."

He didn't sound convincing, so Carly just kept her gaze locked on his, hoping, praying he would cave. She wanted this to come from him. She didn't want to go running to her uncle with what she suspected without hearing it directly from Kyle. Nor did she want to keep this to herself anymore. It wasn't right.

And as her thoughts scrambled over each other, she realized this was precisely what Derek was talking about when he said he hadn't wanted to put this burden on her shoulders.

She was carrying it now, and it was agonizing, confusing, and heartbreaking. It was a no-win situation. And she'd only been in it for a few days.

"I think you do," she said.

Kyle laid his head back, closing his eyes, his hands clenching. "I can't talk about it," he ground out. "It's too hard."

"Why?"

He swept in a long, slow breath, then another, and Carly thought she might have pushed him too far.

"Because I can't go to prison. I just can't." His voice broke into a whimper and he covered his face with his hands.

Carly leaned back, relief blended with sorrow pouring through her.

Then he looked at her. "But keeping this secret, it's so hard. It's so hard."

She didn't know what to say to that. She just stayed where she was, torn between the knowledge of his admission and what it cost him, and what it could mean for Derek.

"Your brother loves you very much," was all she could pull out of her tumbling thoughts. "That's why he did what he did."

"I know. Don't you think I know?" Kyle pressed the palms of his hands against his face, his eyes closed. "I keep figuring if I don't think about it, it will all go away. If I pretend my cancer isn't real, it will all go away. But now I'm in the hospital and I know it's real..." His voice broke and Carly felt a surge of sympathy for him.

He pulled in a steadying breath and lowered his hands, looking down at them. "Mom and Dad and Derek all want me to tell Alia that I'm probably not going to make the end of the year. And that's so hard. I feel like I'm getting pushed into a corner and I don't know where to go. I can't outrun all of this anymore."

To her dismay, she saw the glistening track of tears on his face.

"There's a verse in the Bible that says, 'You will know the truth and the truth will set you free.' It's from John." At one time Carly would have been able to quote chapter and verse, but after Derek went to prison, she'd stopped reading her Bible.

Though it had been her choice, she still felt it was yet another casualty in the battle to protect Kyle.

"But the truth could put me in prison," he said.

"There are many kinds of prisons," Carly said, leaning forward now, taking his hand. "I think you've been living in one for the past four years."

He was quiet a moment, then nodded. "It's been so hard. I keep thinking if I just ignore everything, the cancer, what Derek did for me, the drugs, it'll disappear. But it's always, always there." He looked over at her, his eyes red-rimmed. "And now your uncle Gene is back, and I know he never believed Derek did it. He kept at me so hard. It was easier to lie then. Now, I know he won't quit until he finds out the truth and I don't have the reserves to keep lying."

Carly had no comment on that, because it was true. Uncle Gene as much as admitted that to her himself. "He's retired, you know."

"Those Mounties don't ever retire."

He wasn't too far off about that.

"What do you think I should do?" he asked, his expression bewildered, his eyes fearful.

She was tempted to say *Throw yourself on the mercy of the court*, but she wasn't sure Kyle would see much mercy in that. Not after his brother got three years.

And yet...

"I think cancer isn't the only thing that's killing you," she said, her voice quiet.

Kyle looked away, pensive.

Then the sound of footsteps approaching caught her attention and Kyle's.

It was Louise.

Finally, Carly thought, and yet wished she had more time. She felt as if she had been getting somewhere with Kyle.

"Hello, Carly. Good to see you here already," Louise said. Her gray hair curled around her smiling face. She wore a brown hoodie printed with white leaves. Blue jeans and running shoes. Simple and comfortable. Approachable.

"Hello, Mom," Kyle said with a wan smile.

Louise walked over to the bed, bent over and brushed a kiss over his forehead. "Hello yourself."

Carly always found it curious that Derek never referred to Louise and Thomas as Mom and Dad as easily as Kyle did. Until Derek explained that he and Kyle had been moved around too much. He hadn't trusted that any place would be their final one.

Kyle, however, was younger and more willing to latch on to them as parental figures.

Louise looked around and Carly stood. "You can sit here," she said, pulling her chair away from the bed. "I'll get another chair."

"Thanks, my dear, that would be great."

She moved to sit down as Carly grabbed another chair and brought it close.

As Louise hooked her quilted bag over the back of the chair, she smiled at Carly. "I'm sorry I'm late. My friend Donna Carleton wouldn't let me off the phone. She's still struggling with the death of her husband and needed to talk."

"I'm sure that's been hard for her."

"Yeah, and her sons, Logan and Billy." She gave Carly an apologetic look. "Sorry. Didn't mean to pull you into other drama."

Carly hesitantly sat, curiosity pinging through her. Why did Louise want to meet her here?

"And how is the event center coming?" Louise continued, clearly willing to make some more small talk. "Derek has been

CAROLYNE AARSEN

keeping us updated on the progress. We keep telling him he has to hurry and finish it. We want to hold our fortieth wedding anniversary party there next summer. Invite everyone we know."

And knowing Louise, that was half of Millars Crossing.

"That would be amazing. I'll pencil you in." Carly was willing to go along with the chitchat for now. Louise was a kind, loving person. Carly had always enjoyed spending time with her when she and Derek were dating. Didn't matter when they came, Louise never failed to have cookies or cake or loaf or something sweet to eat with the coffee that was always percolating.

The conversation was always easy. Relaxed. She knew that Louise and Thomas were thrilled that she and Derek were dating. So excited when they announced their engagement.

Louise had offered to help with all the wedding plans, and Carly had gratefully accepted. Not having a sister or a mother was a bit of a handicap, so it was wonderful to have the support. Louise knew everyone in town and had managed to get her deals on catering, flowers, and even the rental of the church for a stand-up tea reception after the service.

But when it came time to cancel, Carly hadn't involved Louise at all. In fact, she had kept her distance.

"And how are you doing?" Louise asked, her eyes holding Carly's as if trying to pin her down. "Really doing?"

Carly wasn't sure what to say. Where to start. She found it curious that Louise would want to have this conversation in Kyle's hospital room.

"I've been better," she said, tired of dancing around things. Tired of pretending everything was okay when it most assuredly wasn't.

"I'm sure you have been." Louise was quiet a moment, glancing over at Kyle, who had pulled his phone out. As if he wanted to blank the two of them out. She turned back to Carly.

180

"I may as well get right to the point. I know you and Derek are, how to say, on the outs?"

"That's one way of saying it," Carly said, then immediately felt small and petty. She blamed it on the weariness that clawed at her. The struggle between what she felt she needed to do and what she preferred.

"He's not been happy lately," Louise said, campaigning for her son.

"Nor have I," Carly said. "It's been hard. Difficult." She shot another glance at Kyle, who was still ignoring both of them. *Regrouping*, Carly thought. Maybe already regretting the things he'd said.

Louise put her hand on Carly's. "I know the truth of what happened with Derek. And I know what you're struggling with." She looked over at Kyle, who shot them a quick glance over the top of his phone but then looked away again. Avoiding them. "And so does Kyle."

"We already talked about that," Kyle muttered.

"And that's why your father and Derek are coming."

Carly's heart rate shot up to dangerous levels. "What?" was all she could muster.

Louise kept her eyes on Kyle as she spoke. "We need to talk things over."

"Shouldn't you do that as a family?" Carly asked, feeling cornered.

"We already did. And Thomas and I knew we needed to wait until Kyle was better and involve you."

"Why?"

Louise pulled her gaze back to Carly. "Because this has affected you as much as anyone else." She pressed her lips together, looking down. "And, well, I'm not above a little manipulating. I know something happened between you and Derek—"

"He lied to me. He kept me in the dark." The words spilled

out, but even as she spoke them aloud in front of Louise and Kyle, she realized how harsh they sounded.

And yet...

"I know, my dear, I know." Louise touched her arm. "We had no idea what was happening, but we know now." Kyle still stared at his phone. But his fingers weren't moving.

"And now I feel like I'm carrying a burden that isn't mine, but I don't know where to put it."

"I could say at the foot of the cross, and knowing you, I'm sure you have."

"Not as easily as I should have," Carly admitted.

"However, that doesn't solve the problem about what to do to put an end to the lies."

Carly pulled in a deep breath and looked at Kyle. This time he was looking at both of them, and he looked beaten. She knew he felt as if he was pressed on every side, and right now, he was.

She was about to say something more when a light knock sounded on the door.

Carly looked up, thinking it was a doctor or a nurse.

Instead, Derek entered the room.

He said nothing, just took a few steps, but it was as if he filled the space with his presence, took it over.

Carly's heart tumbled and turned, and though she wanted to look away, needed to, her eyes slid to his.

For a heartbeat their gazes locked and it was as if the air was sucked out of the room. But Derek was the first to pull away, turning to his brother, nodding at him.

Then Louise smiled at him, as if his presence was completely expected.

"You came," she said.

"You asked me to," he replied.

"This is a total setup," Kyle put in, but he sounded defeated. "And an intervention. Dad's coming too."

Carly sensed he wanted to sound tougher than he felt, but again she saw the fear in his eyes.

"Good thing Kyle doesn't have a roommate," Derek said, his tone dry. "This place is going to get crowded."

"I already spoke to the nurse, and she said it was okay to have more than two visitors, so I've gone through the proper channels. As one does," she said, giving Derek a pointed look.

Carly didn't want to know what that was about.

But she was far too aware of Derek standing beside her. Far too aware of the faint scent of sawdust and diesel that hung around him. He must have come right from work.

She heard slow, measured footsteps, and then Thomas joined them.

"So. Here we are," he said, his voice quiet, his tone steady as he pulled up a chair on the other side of Louise. "We've done enough pussyfooting around. We need to talk." His tone was direct and no-nonsense. "The truth needs to come out now."

Carly couldn't stop herself from looking at Derek. He looked as concerned as Kyle did.

But then their eyes met again, and she didn't miss the look of relief on his face.

Nor the flicker of connection that sparked a responding one in her. She saw him swallow even as he kept his gaze locked on hers. "Are you okay with this?" he asked.

His consideration locked into her soul. She nodded and, to her surprise, he dragged a chair close to her. Quite close. Her knee brushed his and awareness shivered through her.

"So, Kyle, like I said, we need to have a long-overdue discussion," Thomas continued.

Kyle's panicked gaze lit on Carly, then Derek. For a moment Carly thought he might faint again.

But then he laid back, blinked a few times, and nodded. "I know we do," he said, his voice quavering. Broken. "I know."

CHAPTER SEVENTEEN

"*C*an we talk?" Derek asked Carly as they left Kyle's hospital room.

Louise and Thomas stayed behind. They wanted to pray with Kyle as he dealt with the repercussions of what he was about to do.

"Of course," she said. How could she say no after what had just happened?

They stepped outside into the cool night air. The sun had dipped below the horizon. A few vehicles drove past.

"Can we just walk to the river?"

"Sounds good." She didn't want to be where other people would be. They had too much to discuss.

They settled into an easy stroll as they left the hospital. He shortened the stride of his long legs to match hers.

Sitting beside Derek in Kyle's hospital room had been both pleasure and pain. To some degree, she was ashamed of how she'd behaved a few days ago. Of what she had thrown at him previously.

And yet...and yet part of her knew she was justified.

They walked quietly. A few people were out, walking dogs,

pushing fussy babies in buggies. Carly recognized a young woman who'd been a few grades below her in school. They said a quiet hello as they passed each other.

She greeted another couple, both friends of hers.

"Your roots go deep here, don't they?" Derek asked.

She wondered if she imagined the wistful tone in his voice.

"Generations," she said. "Many of them buried in the church cemetery." He knew that, and she guessed he was edging his way to the conversation he wanted to have. Needed to have.

She wasn't sure whether she was supposed to apologize or not.

This was all too confusing.

"It's good to be back here," Carly said, shoving her hands into her pockets, her purse slung across her shoulders.

"I know what you mean." Derek's declaration meant something different than hers did.

A few more minutes of silence but somehow, after they'd all talked to Kyle, she felt less uncomfortable than she thought she would.

"It was good to talk to Kyle," Derek finally said. "And I'm glad you were there as well. What happened had as much to do with you as me."

"I didn't know what the agenda was," Carly admitted. "Which is probably a good thing. I don't know if I would have come otherwise."

"You didn't want to see me?"

Carly eased out a sigh as they made a turn down the hill toward the river path. "I wasn't sure what to say to you. It was easier to just avoid you. I didn't know how to...how to find my way back to you."

"I was always there," he said, his voice holding a gently chiding tone.

"I know. But I was the one who had to figure out what to do

CAROLYNE AARSEN

with what I knew." She pulled in a slow breath. "After the past few days I understand better what you meant."

"As in?"

She said nothing as they walked along the river, trying to pull her thoughts into some cohesive unit. They came to a bench and she sat down, resting her clasped hands on her knees.

"As in the burden of the truth," she finally said. "As in carrying all that and knowing that no matter what I did, it would be a lousy choice. A hard decision. I finally understand why you didn't want to put it on my shoulders. Carrying it the past few days has been hard enough."

"I wanted to tell you everything," he said, his voice laced with pain. Carly turned to him, held his eyes, let his anguish wash over her. "I wanted to let you know, but I couldn't put that responsibility on your shoulders."

"And now I understand why," Carly said. "I would have had to do something with it. Uncle Gene was in the RCMP. He was the one who arrested you. I would have felt duty-bound to tell him."

"Because you're an honorable and honest person. I wouldn't have expected you to hold on to the lie. I couldn't do that. Make you carry that burden. Make you choose. You used to tell me that the truth would set you free, but in my case, the truth would have put Kyle in prison. So, I chose the lie. I chose my brother over you. And I'm sorry that I had to do that. But I can't tell you a lie and say I wouldn't do it again. Or say that I made the wrong choice."

Carly heard the pain in his voice and, as he reiterated things he'd said before, realities she finally understood for herself, something shifted in her.

Derek was a faithful, sacrificing man. He didn't put his own needs first. He put the needs of others first.

The words crashed into her mind, washed over her soul and left, in their wake, a quiet shame.

Yes, she'd been hurt, humiliated, and devastated.

But sitting beside her, opening his heart to her, was an honorable man. A man of integrity, even despite his covering for his brother.

As if sensing her weakening, he moved closer, took her hands in his.

"I agonized over what I had to do. I wanted it all to go away. I was devastated at what I knew my choices would do to you. And it tore me up inside."

His anguish came through in his voice, in how his hands tightened on hers.

"I wish you had told me, even though I understand why you couldn't. Such a hard choice."

"It wasn't because I loved you less," Derek said. "It wasn't because I loved Kyle more."

"He's your brother. You've always had to protect him."

Derek gave a tight nod, acknowledging her comment. "All my life I had to watch out for him. I couldn't separate loving him from loving you. I didn't know how to choose."

She wished she could be a bigger person and say he made the best choice. But she couldn't. Because that choice took him away from her. Broke up their relationship and shattered her heart.

"But you're here now and I'm here now and Kyle—"

"I don't want to talk about Kyle anymore," Derek said. "I've given him enough space in my thoughts and soul. I want to talk about us. You and me."

"I like the sound of that," Carly said, pulling one hand free from his and running it over his face, as if learning him all over again.

Then she noticed again the edge of a tattoo peeking out of his shirt sleeve.

She now felt she had a right to inspect it further, so she slid his shirt up with her forefinger. The tattoo was an intricate cross. "This is new," she said.

"Got it two years ago. From my cellmate."

He spoke the words carefully, as if laying them down in front of her, giving her space to let them settle.

"Was he your cellmate the entire time?"

"Yes. I was lucky. Dayson was a great big guy. No one messed with him, so we hung together."

He paused, giving her a chance to comment. But she had nothing to say. No judgment to make.

"He was, is, a real strong Christian. We would hold Bible studies after hours. During lockdowns. He was a good man. He always reminded me of where my hope lay. Not in the powers of this world or in the so-called success of this world. I clung to that during those times I thought I had no hope."

The bleakness in his voice tore at her heart. The price he had paid for his brother had been too steep.

She kept her hand on his shoulder, her fingers slowly caressing it as if trying to give him some small comfort.

"But the hardest part was knowing that you thought I was a drug dealer. A criminal." Deep pain emanated from his eyes. "I wanted to write you and tell you different, but I couldn't. At one time I wondered if I had done the right thing, but once I was in prison, after just a week, I knew Kyle wouldn't have survived. He was my only blood family and I've always taken care of him." His repetition of what he had said earlier underlined the difficult choices he'd had to make.

Carly tried to imagine herself in the same situation. Tried to think if she would have done the same for any of her brothers.

But it wouldn't gel. She'd never had to stand up for any of her brothers the way Derek had to for Kyle. Had never had to make the tough choices Derek did.

She thought of what Jason had told her about the reason Derek and Kyle had been moved to Millars Crossing.

Because he was protecting Kyle against someone larger and more powerful.

"He was really all you had, right?" Carly asked. The question was almost rhetorical.

"I guess," Derek said. "Until we moved in with the Kennermans. Even then I had a hard time not feeling like I had to watch over him. But then I met you and everything changed. I had someone else I cared for so deeply that the thought of hurting you was like a sledgehammer to my heart. You made me want to be better. You made me want to deserve you. And maybe, deep down, if I let Kyle go to jail, I thought I might disappoint you as well."

Carly held that thought then spooled it out, taking it to the end. Would she have been disappointed if Derek hadn't gone to prison for his brother?

Maybe. Maybe she would.

"It was a no-win situation, I understand that now." Carly gave in to an impulse and threaded her fingers through his thick hair, slipping her other hand around his neck. Anchoring him close to her. "I'm sorry you had to deal with all of this. And even now, it can't be easy knowing what might happen."

"I have to think of what Kyle said just before we left him. 'The truth will set you free.' Said he heard that somewhere."

Carly had to smile but added nothing to the comment. "I think Kyle has been stuck in his own prison the past few years. He's hid behind bluster and denial. He may come across as selfish, but I know he cares deeply about you."

Derek swallowed, nodding. "I know." He closed his eyes and rested his forehead against hers. "I thought we weren't going to talk about Kyle anymore."

"I thought so too, but his life is intertwined with yours. And if you and I are going to get back together, I need to acknowledge that."

"Are we getting back together?" Derek asked quietly, as if he hardly dared expect an answer.

"I hope so," Carly said. "I missed you so much. Having you back and then losing you again, I didn't know how I was going to get through it." She slipped closer to him, hating the distance between them.

"You are an amazing woman," Derek said, holding her tight against him, cradling her head in the crook of his neck. "I love you so much, it scares me."

"Me too. I don't ever want to be apart from you again."

Derek stroked her head over and over as if needing to know she was really there. As if afraid she might suddenly disappear.

Then he tucked his finger under her chin, lifting her face to his.

Carly knew what was next and pulled his head down, their lips meeting, hungry, unquenchable. Their mouths moved in harmony, tasting, touching, experiencing.

She moaned against his mouth, her arms wrapped so tightly around him she thought she was hurting him.

He pulled back and she protested, but he rained kisses on her face, her cheeks, buried his face in her neck.

"I love you," she whispered, drawing back to see his beloved face, to trace the curves of his cheek, his chin, her finger tracing the soft warmth of his lips. "I love you so much."

He held her gaze, his eyes glistening. Was he crying?

This strong, tough, manly man?

"I'm sorry," he whispered, shifting so he could swipe at the tears in his eyes with the cuff of his shirt.

The very unmasculine move dove into her very soul.

If anything, it made her love him more, if that was even possible.

"No. Please don't be sorry."

"It's just, I can't believe this. I can't believe we're together again."

She pressed a quick kiss to his beautiful, passionate mouth, then smiled up at him. "I can't either."

"So, I proposed before all fancy and pretty, but I'm going to just do it simple now. But from the deepest parts of my heart. Carly, will you marry me?"

"Without any hesitation."

He grew serious then. "I won't leave you hanging. I'll be with you every step of the way."

"I know. I'm not worried about that."

He pulled in a sigh and she suspected his thoughts went to the same place hers did.

Kyle.

"I'll be praying for Kyle, you know," she said. "Praying that God will work His will in his life and give him whatever he needs. He's got a rough road ahead of him no matter what, but he has you, the Kennermans, and Jason, and now he has me."

"I know. And he's grown up a lot in the past few days. Hours even." He released a harsh laugh. "I just hope it sticks."

"That's up to him to decide," Carly said.

Derek smiled at her. "You know, I can face whatever will come if I know I've got you beside me."

"Always and in all ways," she assured him.

Then they kissed again, sealing the promise.

"And now I would like to ask the Kennerman family to come forward," Pastor Simons said, his eyes glancing over the congregation, looking for them.

Derek ran his hands over his pants, glancing sidelong at Kyle. Alia sat beside him, her expression serious.

To his surprise, his little brother had spoken with Alia as he, Thomas, and Louise had encouraged him to. Thankfully, Alia told him she would stick with him. Derek wasn't sure she knew what she was signing up for, but who was he to decide that?

Derek stood then, the first to move, but Carly was right with him, taking his hand, giving him an encouraging smile.

They stepped into the aisle but waited as Kyle made his way, holding on to the pew.

He'd been out of the hospital for over a week now, but his steps were halting and unsure.

The beginning of the end, Derek thought with a pang of sorrow.

Carly's hand tightened on his and he wondered if she sensed his pain. Then he glanced sidelong at her, caught her tender expression.

How had he been so blessed to have this amazing woman back with him?

He didn't know the how or why. He just knew he was thanking God every night for this rich blessing.

Kyle took the cane Alia offered him then walked slowly down the aisle. Thomas and Louise were right behind them, Carly and Derek bringing up the rear.

At first Derek had told Carly she didn't need to come with them. He thought she might be ashamed to be a part of this. But she had protested, saying that she was going to be his wife. She was going to promise to be with him all time. And this was one of those times.

So together they made their way to the front of the church. He heard a few muffled whispers, saw some puzzled expressions.

Yeah, it's the Gilbert boys again, he thought. But pushed that down. Overall, people had been welcoming when he came back. Sure, there were a few unfriendly faces, a few people turned away when he came close, but that was to be expected.

Kyle got to the steps in the front and once again Alia was there to help him, Thomas and Louise right behind.

And in that moment Derek realized something that had never struck him before. He didn't have to take sole responsibility for his brother. Sure, he had known that on some level before, but now, seeing Thomas and Louise help Kyle up the stairs, give him an encouraging hug as he and Carly joined them, eased some of the weight he had been carrying so long.

Maybe not eased it so much as made him realize it wasn't necessary to take it all on.

Kyle pulled a piece of paper out of his pocket. The paper trembled as he unfolded it and set it on the pulpit, his hands shaking as he smoothed it down.

Derek turned to face the congregation, his eyes scanning the crowd, forcing himself to hold his head up. *You have nothing to be ashamed of,* he reminded himself.

Then he saw Gene Sutton. He was frowning, looking as puzzled and curious as the rest of the Sutton family. Carly obviously hadn't told them what was happening today.

Kyle cleared his throat, shot a sidelong glance at Thomas and Louise, then at him and Carly. Alia tucked her arm in Kyle's, smiling her encouragement

"I'm sure..." Kyle hesitated, cleared his throat, and started again. "I'm sure you're all wondering what I'm doing up here." He pulled in a deep breath. "I'm sure you all know that the doctors have diagnosed me with brain cancer. But I don't know if all of you know that it's terminal." Kyle's voice shook as he delivered this information. Derek saw a few sorrowful faces, a few hands rise to mouths as if to hold their reaction in. He turned his attention back to his brother just as Carly slipped her hand through his arm, tucking herself against him. He returned the pressure, chancing a quick look at her then back to his brother.

"But that's not the only reason I'm up here," Kyle continued. "I'm here because I've been told that confession is good for the soul. A wise woman told me that the Bible says, 'You will know the truth and the truth will set you free.' Well, she also told me I've been a prisoner the past few years, but in a worse way than Derek was. And it's true." At this Kyle turned to Derek and gave him a wan smile. "My brother, Derek, has always been there for me. Always stood up for me. You can see he's much bigger than me, so that was always good. Especially all the times we had to start in a new school and kids would pick on me. He would help me out. Sometimes he got into trouble for it. Sorry, bro," Kyle said with an apologetic shrug.

Kyle held Derek's gaze for a heartbeat, then looked at the paper in front of him. "Now you need to know that there was another time Derek got into trouble because of me. You know that over three and some change years ago he was arrested for possession of cocaine. Only it wasn't his. It was mine. All mine." Kyle paused a moment and took in a deep, slow breath. He chanced a quick look up at the congregation when he heard the surprised gasps. "Yeah. I know. Big surprise," he agreed. "And big mistake. But I had already been diagnosed with brain cancer and the doc said I might live two years, maybe three. Guess I proved him wrong." He gave a forced laugh, leaning heavily on the pulpit. "I thought I could maybe sell the drugs and find a treatment in Mexico. Selfish, I know. It was wrong. I know that too. I was scared and desperate."

Another breath and another pause. Derek wondered if Kyle could hold up long enough. But he forced himself to stay where he was as Thomas and Louise moved closer and Carly squeezed his arm just a little tighter.

"Gene Sutton came onto the yard and found the cocaine in Derek's truck. I was freaking out, but Derek took the blame. Said the drugs were his. And I let him. I went along with the lie because I was spit-scared I would go to prison. Derek told me I would die there, and he was right. So I just let him take the blame. I said nothing. And it's been bugging me ever since. Not as much as it should sometimes. I ain't no saint. But lately, it's been more. I know he broke up with Carly before he left. They were gonna get married, and leaving her tore him up inside." He paused and shot another glance at Derek and Carly. "I'm so sorry that happened. You two were meant for each other." He turned back to the congregation. "Anyhow, they're back together, so that's good. I'm still dealing with cancer. And I still don't know how long I have. The doc says not much longer, so I guess we'll see. Anyhow, that's my story, and it's not pretty. I'm not proud of what I did and didn't say. Of letting my brother lose three years of his life because of me. Of having you all think he's some kind of criminal when he's the best brother I could ever ask for. The best guy in my life and the best thing that's happened to me." He seemed to catch himself and then looked at Alia. "You are too, babe. But in a different way."

Her smile told him she forgave him, and Derek once again wondered how his brother found someone like her.

Same way you found someone like Carly.

God's grace.

"Anyhow, I'm done with my little sermon. I'm scared and nervous and I...I'm hoping you can forgive me too." He stopped, and as he folded up his paper, he seemed to remember something. He leaned into the microphone. "And I know I should have said this first, but if you could pray for me, that would be awesome."

This elicited a few cautious smiles.

Then he shoved the paper in his pocket, took his cane, and made his painful way back down the aisle. He kept his head down but Derek could see the looks of sympathy on a few faces. He felt choked up and more emotional than he thought he would be.

It was all out in the open now. It was the end of one part of his life, and the beginning of another.

His and Carly's.

And Kyle's.

He wasn't sure he wanted to envision where Kyle's journey would take him.

One day, one step at a time, he reminded himself. Words that got him through three years in prison now stood him in good stead. That and the prayers of people who cared.

Pastor Simons came to the front and thanked Kyle for what was a difficult moment, then announced the final song of the service.

The congregation rose, the pianist played the first few chords, and Derek felt melancholy as he recognized the song. It was Dayson's favorite. He would hum it or sing it when he could and had taught it to Derek.

He sang along, the words settling into his soul, giving him comfort.

"My strength is found through Christ alone,
The rock in my life, this strong cornerstone."

He sang the song to the end and when it was over, he bent his head, sending up a prayer for strength and peace.

Then he turned to Carly, who was smiling up at him.

"Thanks for being up there with me and my family," he said.

"Of course," she said. "I'm a part of it now too. And I'll be praying for Kyle as well."

He wanted to kiss her right then and there, but that would have to wait.

For now, there were other things ahead of them.

A few people stopped to talk to Kyle, who was still sitting in the pew, waiting for people to finish exiting the church so he wouldn't hold anyone up as he left. He nodded and shook hands and thanked people.

There were a few condemning looks, and Derek knew he couldn't fault anyone their reaction. What Kyle had done was huge. There would have been devastating repercussions for kids in the town and their families had Kyle's plan to sell the cocaine gone through.

"This changes things." Finn and Reuben stood at the end of the pew as Derek and Carly were about to leave.

Derek paused, held his head high but at the same time swallowed a knot of trepidation. He glanced to see if Wyatt was going to join them.

"It does, and can we not talk about this right now?" Carly asked, clinging to Derek's arm. "We want to talk to you at home. Without other...other people around." Carly waved one hand at the people still exiting the church.

"You're right," Reuben agreed. He put his hand on Carly's shoulder and gave it a gentle squeeze then looked over at Derek, his expression serious. "Thanks for what you just did. With your brother. That can't have been easy for any of you."

"It wasn't," Derek admitted.

"Anyhow, Carly is right. We can talk about this later," Finn added. "But I just want to say how thankful I am for the both of you that the truth came out. Wasn't what I expected but then, I'm not always on top of things."

"I'll say," Reuben added, giving his brother a nudge. He looked over at Derek again, a careful smile curling his lips. "Look forward to talking to you at home."

His words were simple but they conveyed an easy acceptance.

And it warmed his heart.

As they walked away, Carly tugged on his arm. "Let's get out of here. If we go out the other way we can avoid more people."

"Sounds good to me."

Then, to his dismay, just as he and Carly were ready to exit the building, Gene Sutton was there in the doorway. His clipped hair, impeccably tailored suit, cinched tie, and military bearing gave him an intimidating look.

Derek glanced behind him to see where Kyle was but thankfully he, Alia, Thomas, and Louise were now walking out of the church, going in another direction.

"So, big revelation," Gene said.

"Uncle Gene, does this have to happen now?" Carly asked, her voice holding a note of impatience. "I want to get home."

He glanced at her and shrugged. "You don't even know what's happening," he said.

Then he looked back at Derek. "I just want to say that I admire you. I admire your willingness to sacrifice yourself for the sake of your brother. That's true love in action."

Derek wasn't sure what to say and, he had to admit, wasn't sure where Gene was going either.

"I know you're probably thinking that I'm following through on the hunch I had all along," Gene continued, rubbing his chin, looking pensive. "I always guessed you weren't the one. I knew my niece would never have been involved with a drug dealer. But you gave me nothing and your brother, well, what can I say. Good actor. Had me fooled." His eyes held Derek's and, to Derek's surprise, his gruff expression softened. "But I think he's sincere now. And I'm sorry he's dealing with all that."

"What are you going to do about this?" Derek couldn't keep the question to himself, wondering why Gene had sought them out now. In church.

"I know this has been weighing heavy on your mind," Gene said, resting his hands on his hips, moving a little closer. "And I know your brother is probably terrified of what might happen to him. But even I can see he's not long for this world. I'm not a Mountie anymore, but I still know the captain here. Good friend of mine. I'm sure I can convince him to investigate all the angles, leave no stone unturned, et cetera, et cetera. Make sure that his reports are all solid. You know, the usual grinding bureaucracies that can slow investigations to a crawl."

He stopped, and Derek knew what he was saying. He would buy enough time for Kyle to die outside of prison. He fought down another knot of sorrow and clung to Carly's hand, deeply thankful for her support and love.

Gene gave both of them a tight smile. "And it's good to see you two together again," he said. "Carly is certainly a lot happier than the last time I saw her."

"Thanks, Uncle Gene," Carly said. She released Derek's arm and gave her uncle a quick hug.

He returned the hug, then without another word, strode off.

Derek wasn't sure what he was allowed to think. Wasn't sure if he should be relieved or not.

"Did that just happen?" he asked.

"It did. He's a good man."

Derek had to agree.

"And soon he'll be your uncle Gene too," Carly said with a flirty smile. "And you know, that will help too."

Derek gave her a hug. "Okay. That was kind of surreal."

"I think we should go back to your parents' place and let them know what else is happening."

"And when do we break the news?"

"About our engagement or the fact that we're going to elope?"

"Both I guess."

"I think the sooner the better."

"And your brothers? Won't they be upset about that?"

Carly shrugged. "They helped me haul all kinds of wedding stuff to the hall the first time, then haul it all back. I'm sure they'll be relieved not to have to do it all over again."

She frowned at him, then stroked his face. "And don't you dare feel badly about that. It wasn't your fault."

"A little bit."

She held up a thumb and forefinger, spacing them about an inch apart. "Maybe a tad."

He was surprised she could joke about that.

"And you're okay with that? Okay with no fancy wedding

with everyone around?" They had talked about it endlessly for the past week, but he still had to make sure.

She grew serious, glancing around the now-empty church. "All the years we went to church here, I imagined myself walking down this aisle in a beautiful white dress. I had it all planned, down to the last flower and piece of ribbon. But you know, I've realized that it doesn't matter. All that fuss and bother." She took his hand. "I had my plans, but now I have you. And that's more important to me than any fancy wedding. I want to be married to you. I want us to start our life as soon as possible."

Relief surged through him as she eased away his concerns. Again.

She walked out of the pew and glanced back at him, her eyes twinkling as he followed her.

"Besides, this way I can beat all my brothers to the altar."

His laugh echoed through the church as they walked down the aisle.

Together.

Thanks for reading. I hope you enjoyed Derek, and Carly's story. Your time in Millars Crossing doesn't need to end, however,

You can spend more time there when you meet Logan and Sarah.

Here's an excerpt from their story:

CAROLYNE AARSEN

A Family's
CHRISTMAS

LOVE IN MILLARS CROSSING BOOK ONE

Thirty-six minutes to go. And though Sarah Westerveld had been driving west for five days to get to her old hometown of Millars Crossing, she needed every second of those thirty-six minutes to compose herself before meeting her father.

She tapped her fingers on the steering wheel in time to the song blasting from the radio and waited at the town's single stoplight. Not much had changed in the six years she had been gone. The bakery, the bank, the drugstore and the flower shop still anchored the four corners of the main street. Just down from the bakery was her cousin's coffee shop, a rare new addition to Millars Crossing.

And the place she had arranged to meet her father.

Since she had moved away, she had received an envelope from him on the first of every month, his decisive handwriting on the outside, a check inside.

And nothing else. No letter. No note. Nothing to show that this came from her father.

A few weeks ago, however, instead of the check, inserted in

the envelope was a single piece of paper with the words "Come Home. I need to talk to you" written on it.

When she phoned to find out what he wanted, he kept the call short, as he always did, and businesslike, as he always did. He said he wanted to tell her what he had to, face-to-face.

Her father wanted to meet her at home, but after all this time, she had no desire to visit with him in that large empty house echoing with memories. So they had arranged to meet at her cousin Janie's coffee shop. Neutral ground, and not far from his office.

A horn honked behind her and Sarah jumped. The light had turned green. She gunned her car through the intersection and slid over the snow and into the lone parking spot down the block from her cousin's coffee shop. Obviously Mr. Kennerman, the street maintenance man, was still around, and still not on the job.

She wound her scarf around her throat and pulled out a toque, jamming it over her long, blond hair before stepping from the warm confines of her car into the crisp winter weather.

I missed this, Sarah thought, tugging on a pair of gloves. Missed the bite of the cold, the invigorating freshness of the chilly air. Sarah pulled back the cuff of her glove.

Thirty-five minutes to go.

She had planned to stay at her cousin's. Her father hadn't objected when she told him. Still, she wasn't sure if it was because he understood why, or because he simply didn't want her in the family house either.

Sarah locked her car and glanced down the road. The trees, now bare, reached farther over the street than she remembered. One of the older buildings in town had been renovated to its original glory. Flags, hanging from new streetlights, drifted in the cool breeze that scuttled rivulets of snow across the street.

The town was busy this early in the day. Busy for Millars

Crossing, which meant most of the parking spots on Main Street were taken. A few people wandered down the sidewalks, their conversation punctuated by puffs of steam. Sarah shivered as she hurried along the path toward the coffee shop, anticipation fluttering through her at the thought of seeing her cousin after all this time.

The door of the coffee shop swung open and a man stepped out.

Dark was the first thought that came to mind. Dark eyebrows. Dark hair. A lean jaw shadowed by whiskers. Angular features molded in a look that both challenged and engaged all comers. His coffee-brown hair brushed the collar of a faded canvas coat open to reveal a denim jacket and sweatshirt. Brown eyes swept over her and Sarah's heart did a slow turn in her chest.

Logan Carleton.

Logan of the scribbles in her notebook, the long, slow looks across the gymnasium and stolen kisses that still haunted her.

Logan of the Across the River Carletons of whom her father couldn't speak without risking a coronary. Which, in turn, had given the broodingly handsome Logan an additional forbidden appeal.

An appeal that only grew when they secretly started dating.

He still had it, she thought as she met the eyes she thought held no sway over her anymore. But old emotions flickered deep within her and the six years she'd been gone slipped away as easily as a young girl's tears.

Six years ago all he'd had to do was send her that crooked smile across the cab of his truck and her heart would do the same slow turn it just had.

Sarah put the brakes on those silly, schoolgirl thoughts. She was older now. Wiser. Harder. She had left Millars Crossing with tears in her eyes because of this man. Now, after all this time, just seeing him could bring forth feelings she thought she had reconciled into her past.

And then, thankfully, his mouth lifted in a faintly cynical smile negating the connection.

"Sarah Westerveld. So you've come back west." The tone in his voice was cooler than the freezing air.

"Hello, Logan," she said quietly. In a town as small as Millars Crossing, this first meeting was inevitable. She just hadn't counted on it being five minutes after her arrival.

"You remembered who I am." He lifted one eyebrow in a mocking gesture. "I'm surprised."

His tone cut. But life and time away from Millars Crossing had changed her. She wasn't the girl who longed for his approval. Needed his smile.

"I was sorry to hear about your father's death." She had stayed in touch with her friends and family here, so she knew.

Logan's eyes narrowed and for a moment she thought she had crossed an unseen line.

"Me too," he growled. "He had a hard life."

"That he did." And Sarah knew part of the blame for that difficulty could be laid at her father's door.

Nine years ago, Jack Carleton had been falsely accused of murdering his business partner. The lengthy trial had scandalized the community and, even though Jack had been exonerated, the verdict hadn't stopped Frank, Sarah's father, from canceling his gravel-crushing contract with Jack. This in turn created the animosity between Frank and Jack that Sarah grew up with but couldn't completely understand.

"I heard you took over your father's gravel business," Sarah continued, determined to act as if meeting Logan was no different than meeting any other high school acquaintance. She had a hard time looking at him, so she focused on the top button of his jacket. "How is that going for you?"

Logan gave a short laugh. "It's going to be better."

Sarah couldn't stop her attention from flying upward at the harsh tone of his voice.

"So how long are you around for this time?" he continued.

"I'm here to visit my father. That's all."

"That's all? I shouldn't be surprised, should I?" He held her gaze a heartbeat longer, then stepped past her and walked away.

Just as she had walked away from him six years ago.

As Sarah watched him, his hands tucked in the pocket of his canvas coat, his whole demeanor one of a man in charge of his world, she felt her heart twist with pain. Logan had always had a strong self-confidence, which had served him well amid the whispers and innuendos during his father's trial.

It was that self-assurance to which Sarah had been drawn. Unfortunately, Sarah had not possessed the same confidence while they were dating; she had insisted they keep their relationship secret. And they had. For the entire eight months. And then her father, who had never disguised his active dislike for the Carleton family, found out.

Sarah pushed open the door to the shop, shivering in the warmth and letting the welcoming scent of ground coffee beans draw her back to the present. She wasn't here to reminisce over old flames. She had a job to do, plain and simple.

As the door sighed closed behind her, she drew in a slow breath, willing her heart to stop its erratic beating.

"Sarah. You're here!" A high-pitched squeal pierced the low murmur of the customers in the coffee bar.

Janie Corbett threaded her way through the people perched at high stools and tables, her arms outstretched, her Westerveld blue eyes wide with excitement. With great relief, Sarah walked into her cousin's embrace, letting Janie's arms pull her tightly close.

Janie patted Sarah's cheeks, her smile threatening to split her face. "Look at you. All grown-up and even skinnier than ever. And I love the longer hairstyle," Janie said, flicking her fingers through Sarah's shoulder-length curls. "Looks elegant. Refined."

"Well, I'm not. Refined or elegant, that is."

"Not the way you play basketball." Janie adjusted the bandanna holding her own pale blond hair back from her face. "I heard that Uncle Morris and Ethan saw you in action in Calgary, at some university competition."

Sarah remembered and smiled. Seeing her uncle and cousin's familiar faces after the game had been a bright spot in her life. "That wasn't my best game."

Sarah followed Janie to the counter, glancing around the shop as she did. She saw a few familiar faces but could tell from the slightly puzzled frowns sent her way that her own face wasn't ringing any bells.

"They were still pretty impressed," Janie said, pulling out a large mug. She gave Sarah a quick smile. "I'm so glad you're here."

"I am too." Sarah released a gentle sigh as she perched on an empty stool. She folded her arms on the granite countertop as she took in the bright and cheery decor. "This looks great, Janie. You did a fantastic job."

"Well, Aunty Dot helped me with the design and Uncle Dan and Uncle Morris rounded up all the cousins to do the heavy work."

Sarah glanced up above the coffee machines to the chalkboard filled with pink and green swirling script describing the menu for the day. "And the good people of Millars Crossing are really ready for espressos, cappuccinos and flavored macchiatos?"

"Honey, they are lapping it up."

"From cups I would hope."

Janie gave her a blank look, then laughed. "Very funny."

"You walked right into it." Sarah smiled and glanced at her

watch while her stomach did another flip. Twenty-nine minutes left.

"You want something now, or do you want to wait for your dad?"

"I'll have a hot chocolate."

"And when are you coming over?"

"When I'm done here."

"Your dad wasn't really impressed with the fact that you're staying with me, but I told him that I wasn't going to get involved." With a hiss of compressed air and quick, practiced movements, Janie layered thick whipping cream on top of the steaming cup of hot chocolate and carried it around the counter. "Let's sit by the window."

She waved away the cash Sarah pulled out of her purse. "On the house. Consider it a temptation to stay longer."

"I hope you don't do this for all the Westervelds," Sarah said as she settled in at the table Janie led her to.

"I'd be broke if I did that."

Sarah angled her cousin a quick smile then scooped up a dollop of whipped cream and popped it into her mouth with a sigh of satisfaction. Fat. The main ingredient in all good comfort food. Bring it on.

"So. Three weeks." Janie leaned her elbows on the table. "What ever made you decide on that puny length of time?"

"It's longer than the two weeks I had originally planned." Sarah knew this conversation was a trial run for the many she suspected she would have with other family.

"I guess we were hoping we could convince you to stay longer, but my mom said you've got your escape ticket booked." Janie gave her a penetrating look, as if trying to push past the defenses Sarah hastily erected.

"What? A girl can't go traveling?"

"You've definitely got the family in a dither. We're all trying to figure out why, after being gone so long after finishing school and graduating, you're only here awhile." The hurt in Janie's voice teased out memories. Sarah had grown up with cousins and aunts and uncles all of whom had staked the claim of heredity on her life. Though she owed them collectively more than she could ever repay, she had hoped her current stay would cover some of the emotional debt. But to the Westervelds, if you didn't live within twenty minutes of Millars Crossing, you were "away" and if you were "away" you had better make sure that you made the pilgrimage at least for Easter, Christmas or Thanksgiving.

But in spite of the pull of some family's heredity and expectations, Sarah had stayed away, and her father had never extended any kind of invitation.

Until now.

"And what's with this, not sticking around until Christmas?" Janie pressed.

"Christmas is not my favorite season." This was her catchall comment when people back at the college would ask every year if she was going home for the holidays. Most people accepted that at face value and didn't pry. But here in Millars Crossing, people didn't have to pry. Most of them knew.

"I'm sorry." Janie's teasing look slipped off her face to be replaced by sorrow. "It's been six years since Marilee died, hasn't it?"

"Six years on the twenty-third of December." Sarah swallowed down an unexpected knot of pain she thought had eased away.

"You know we all lost something that day," Janie said, reaching over and covering Sarah's hand with her own. "I just wish you could have let us help you through it all. You left so soon afterward. I'm sure your father missed you."

And Sarah was sure he didn't. Other than a terse phone call once a year on her birthday, she had instigated every connection between them. Every phone call, every letter. She had spent her whole life trying to please her father and in the end, her slavish devotion had turned out to be like pouring light into a black hole. She could never give enough to fill it.

Because Sarah was not Marilee, and Marilee was not here.

"Well, I'm here now."

"I guess we were all hoping you'd want to spend some time here. I mean, it's like you've wiped away all our years of family and visiting and holidays." Janie waved her hand, the casual gesture underlining the hurt in her words. "And then you only come back for three weeks."

"C'mon Janie," Sarah protested. "I wrote you every week, posted on your blog, checked out the cousins' MySpace sites, phoned..."

"A face-to-face visit would have been nice."

"I know." But a face-to-face visit would have meant seeing her father again, something she had avoided ever since that horrible confrontation after Marilee's funeral.

Even coming here had been fraught with second thoughts and fears that she was simply slipping back into the role of the good daughter.

She had worked so hard to get where she was. After a couple of lost years of dithering, she had settled on an education degree. Now that she had graduated, she had a job waiting for her in Toronto, teaching at an all-girl's school, a prestigious coup. She looked forward to applying all the things she had learned. But first, this trip she and her friends had planned since they first met two years ago—six months backpacking through Europe.

"I don't suppose you could change the ticket?"

Sarah was spared yet another explanation when Janie glanced sideways and straightened, her one hand drifting up to her hair in a preening gesture. "I wondered when Logan would remember his work gloves."

Sarah wasn't going to look, the very sound of his name

sending a shiver of apprehension chasing down her spine but as Janie got up to get the gloves her head moved of its own accord. And she saw Logan pause in the process of opening the frost-encrusted glass door to the coffee shop. He was looking back over his shoulder. An older man coming out of the bank across the street had caught his attention.

Her father. Frank Westerveld.

And he was coming here. From the tight look on her father's face, Sarah could tell he was not one bit happy to see Logan Carleton.

Her father's tailored wool coat, crisp white shirt and silk tie were an elegant contrast to the canvas coat, stained jean jacket and faded blue jeans of the younger man who had turned to face him.

Sarah found herself clenching her fists as she watched Logan, the man she had once dated, face down her father, the man who had demanded they stop. Her father was talking... Logan replying. But while her father stabbed the air with his finger as if punctuating his words, Logan kept his hands in his pockets when he spoke; the picture of nonchalance.

"Oh boy," Janie murmured, returning. "This will not turn out well."

"Some things haven't changed," Sarah said with a sigh, watching her father, remembering his fury when he found out that she had been seeing the rugged young man. It would seem her father's latent anger with her old boyfriend hadn't abated one jot in spite of Sarah having fallen in with her father's wishes.

"I didn't expect to be facing both my dad and Logan as soon as I got here."

"Looks like Logan doesn't want his gloves after all," Janie said.

Sarah turned in time to see Logan salute her father, then turn away, his coat still open.

Her father stood with his back to the shop, his hands clenched into fists at his side.

"Doesn't look as if Logan's gained any more points with your dad," Janie said.

"Logan has never been concerned with points, or my father's opinion," Sarah murmured. "Or anyone else's for that matter."

"Oh c'mon. I know there was a time he cared what *you* thought," Janie said, giving Sarah a playful poke.

"Not for very long." Sarah pulled her attention away from Logan's retreating figure.

The door jangled, heralding some new customers, but still her father stood outside.

"You'd better see to your customers. I should go say hi to my dad, let him know I'm here." Sarah got up and, before she knew what was happening, Janie caught her in a quick, hard hug. "I'm so glad you're back."

Sarah felt a flood of sentiment for her brusque and straightforward cousin.

The hug felt better than she remembered.

Janie drew back and patted her awkwardly on her shoulder. "I'll see you on Sunday? At church?"

She felt it again. The gentle tug of expectations. She knew the drill. If you were a Westerveld and you were in town on Sunday, showing up at church was mandatory. But Sarah, who used to love church, hadn't been since she left Millars Crossing. However, though she had let the faith of her childhood slip, she couldn't completely eradicate the notion that God did still have some small hold on her life.

And there was the guilt. Always a good motivator.

"Yeah. I'll be there."

"You'll have to be or you'll have all the aunties calling you up demanding to know if you're sick. Or dead." Janie stopped, her eyes growing wide, then pressed her hand to her mouth. "I'm sorry," she said behind her fingers. "Wasn't thinking."

"Don't worry about it." Sarah stroked her cousin's arm to reassure her.

But Janie wasn't looking at her. "What...something's wrong."

The frightened note in Janie's voice made Sarah look up in time to see her father's head drop, his gloved hand pressed against the window, his other hanging by his side.

She moved, her chair clattering to the floor behind her. Her feet wouldn't move fast enough. She burst out of the coffee shop in time to keep her father from falling to the sidewalk.

When she regained her senses, she realized Logan had also seen what had happened and returned.

"Here. I got him," he said, catching Sarah's father under his arms.

But Frank pushed Logan's hand away, his face growing red. "Go away, Carleton."

"Call nine-one-one," Logan said, ignoring Frank's warning. "Use my cell phone," Logan ordered. "Coat pocket. Right side."

Sarah hesitated only a moment, then dug into Logan's jacket and pulled out the small phone.

Her father pushed at Logan, his breath coming in short gasps of distress. "I asked you." He glanced at Sarah. "I asked him..."

"I'll hold him. You call," Sarah said, holding out the phone to Logan while her father pushed at him with increasing clumsiness.

"Why? Logan. Why?" Her father's speech grew slurred, his eyes unfocused.

What was going on?

Whatever it was, her father seemed more distressed about Logan's presence than about what was happening to him.

"Dad. I'm here." Sarah pushed Logan's hand away, slipping her arm under her father.

She put her finger on her father's neck, not knowing what she should be doing but knowing that she had to keep Logan away from her father because his presence wasn't helping him calm down at all. "Dad. Look at me. What is happening? Does your chest hurt? Is the pain going down your arm?"

He shook his head, his eyes growing wide.

Oh dear Lord, not now, she thought, helplessness washing over her in a wave. Not after all these years. He had to tell me something. Had to say something. Don't take that away from me.

Sarah's prayer was instinctive, a hearkening back to a time when she thought God listened.

But her father's angry focus was on Logan, who was barking directions into his cell phone.

"Logan..." Frank tried to lift his arm, but it fell back to his side.

His speech grew increasingly slurred.

"Never mind him, Dad. Talk to me. Look at me," she called, trying desperately to get him to even glance her way.

He took a breath and Sarah caught his head as it slumped to the side, turning his face to her. But even as Sarah tried to catch his attention, Frank Westerveld's entire focus was on Logan Carleton.

And then his eyes fell shut.

"Dad. *Talk to me,*" she called out, frantic.

To find out more click, on the cover below:

OTHER SERIES

I have many other books for you to enjoy. Check them out here.

FAMILY BONDS

#1 SEEKING HOME

A rancher who suffered a tragic loss. A single mother on the edge. Can these two find the courage to face a romantic new beginning?

#2 CHOOSING HOME

If you like emergency room drama, second chances, and quaint small-town settings, then you'll adore this romance.

#3 COMING HOME

He thought she chose a hotel over him. She thought he loved money more than her. Years later, can they fill the emptiness in their hearts?

#4 FINDING HOME

She's hiding a terrible truth. He's trying to overcome his scandalous history. Together, forgiveness might give them a second chance.

FAMILY TIES

Four siblings trying to finding their way back to family and faith

A COWBOY'S REUNION

He's still reeling from the breakup. She's ashamed of what she did. Can a chance reunion mend the fence, or are some hearts forever broken? If you like second chance stories, buried passions, and big country settings, then you'll love this emotional novel.

"I enjoyed this book and had trouble putting it down and had to finish it.

If the rest of this series is this great, I look forward to reading more books by Carolyne Aarsen." Karen Semones - Amazon Review

THE COWBOY'S FAMILY

She's desperate. He's loyal. Will a dark lie hold them back from finding love on the ranch? If you like determined heroines, charming cowboys, and family dramas, then you'll love this heartfelt novel.

"What a wonderful series! The first book is Cowboy's Reunion. Tricia's story begins in that book. Emotional stories with wonderful characters. Looking forward to the rest of the books in this series." Jutzie - Amazon reviewer

TAMING THE COWBOY

A saddle bronc trying to prove himself worthy to a father who never loved him. A wedding planner whose ex-fiancee was too busy chasing his own dreams to think of hers. Two people, completely wrong for each other who yet need each other in ways they never realized. Can they let go of their own plans to find a way to heal together?

"This is the third book in the series and I have loved them all. . . . can't wait to see what happens with the last sibling." - Amazon reviewer

THE COWBOY'S RETURN

The final book in the Family Ties Series:

He enlisted in the military, leaving his one true love behind.

She gave herself to a lesser man and paid a terrible price.

In their hometown of Rockyview, they can choose to come together or say a final goodbye...

"This author did an amazing job of turning heartache into happiness with realism and inspirational feeling." Marlene - Amazon Reviewer

SWEETHEARTS OF SWEET CREEK

Come back to faith and love

#1 HOMECOMING

Be swept away by this sweet romance of a woman's search for belonging and second chances and the rugged rancher who helps her heal.

#2 - HER HEARTS PROMISE

When the man she once loved reveals a hidden truth about the past, Nadine has to choose between justice and love.

#3 - CLOSE TO HIS HEART

Can love triumph over tragedy?

#4 - DIVIDED HEARTS

To embrace a second chance at love, they'll need to discover the truths of the past and the possibilities of the future...

#5 - A HERO AT HEART

If you like rekindled chemistry, family drama, and small, beautiful towns, then you'll love this story of heart and heroism.

#6 - A MOTHER'S HEART

If you like matchmaking daughters, heartfelt stories of mending broken homes, and fixer-upper romance, then this story of second chances is just right for you.

HOLMES CROSSING SERIES

The Only Best Place is the first book in the Holmes Crossing Series.

#1 THE ONLY BEST PLACE

One mistake jeopardized their relationship. Will surrendering her dreams to save their marriage destroy her?

#2 ALL IN ONE PLACE

She has sass, spunk and a haunting secret.

#3 THIS PLACE

Her secret could destroy their second chance at love

#4 A SILENCE IN THE HEART

Can a little boy, an injured kitten and a concerned vet with his own past pain, break down the walls of Tracy's heart?

#5 ANY MAN OF MINE

Living with three brothers has made Danielle tired of guys and cowboys. She wants a man. But is she making the right choice?

#6 A PLACE IN HER HEART

Her new boss shattered her dreams and now she has to work with him. But his vision for the magazine she loves puts them at odds. Can they find a way to work together or will his past bitterness blind him to future love.

Made in the USA
Monee, IL
19 January 2022

89421135R00132